W9-DEK-567

COUNTER CLOCKWISE

JASON COCKCROFT

KATHERINE TEGEN BOOKS
An Imprint of HarperCollins*Publishers*

TO LISA, FOR HER PATIENCE

Counter Clockwise
 For information address HarperCollins Children's Books, a division of HarperCollins Publishers, 1350 Avenue of the Americas, New York, NY 10019.
www.harpercollinschildrens.com

Library of Congress Cataloging-in-Publication Data

Cockcroft, Jason.
Counter Clockwise / Jason Cockcroft. — 1st ed.
p. cm.
Summary: With the aid of Bartleby, an enormous Tower of London guard known as a Beefeater, Nathan travels through time to stop his father from changing the past.
ISBN 978-0-06-125554-0 (trade bdg.)
ISBN 978-0-06-125555-7 (lib. bdg.)
[1. Space and time—Fiction. 2. Time travel—Fiction. 3. Fathers and sons—Fiction. 4. London (England)—Fiction. 5. England—Fiction.] I. Title. II. Title: Counterclockwise.
PZ7.C6399 Co 2009 2008022632
[Fic]—dc22 CIP
AC

Drawings by Jason Cockcroft
Typography by Joel Tippie
1 2 3 4 5 6 7 8 9 10

First Edition

CONTENTS

The Moving Fin
Moves on; nor a
Shall lure it back
Nor all your Tea

Time flies like the
Fruit flies like ban

–

CHAPTER ONE

THE BUS

When Nathan's father told him the news, his voice seemed lost in the quiet of the schoolroom—*as though it didn't belong,* Nathan thought.

Nathan couldn't remember his father, Henry, having ever visited the school before. Not for parents' evenings, or school plays. Not even when he and Nathan's mom were still married. That's why when Nathan saw Henry's car arrive at the school gates, he knew something terrible had happened. By the time his teacher, Miss Feather, called Nathan into the school office, Henry was already waiting for him, his face as gray and crumpled as his tie.

"Nathan, it's your mother," Henry began. "She's been in an accident."

Henry waited for Nathan to say something, but Nathan was silent. He couldn't speak. His mouth was dry, and he felt a numbing ache against his forehead, as though a cold fist were pressing down on him.

"She was hit by a bus," Henry continued. "The driver didn't see her until it was too late."

Nathan hesitated. "But she's okay?"

"No, Nathan. No. I'm afraid she's not."

The fist pressed down harder, and Nathan felt hot tears prick his eyes. It had been only a few hours since he'd last seen her. As he was leaving for school, she'd kissed him once on the cheek; then she'd pulled on her coat—the green one Henry had bought her for her birthday. She was leaving too, and so they walked out of the house together. The last thing his mom had said to him was not to come home too late because they had plans for the evening.

"But we're going out tonight," Nathan told Henry, remembering. "We're going to see a movie. We'd planned it," he added, trying to make Henry understand—Henry knew how much Nathan's mom loved the movies.

Miss Feather was standing with Nathan. When he began to cry, she took hold of his hand, trying to comfort him, but Nathan didn't want her holding his hand. He didn't want her, and he didn't want Henry. He wanted his mother.

"We're going to the movies—*tonight*!" he told them.

"Nathan. Your mom's dead, son," Henry said, grabbing Nathan's arm. "Do you understand? She's gone."

"No—she's not! She can't be!"

He couldn't believe she was dead. He didn't *want* to believe it. He didn't want to think that he'd never see her again. Never hug her, or—

"It's a mistake," he said. "It has to be a mistake."

"I'm afraid it's no mistake, Nathan. She's dead. I'm . . . I'm sorry."

Nathan shook his head. But no matter how much he wanted to believe Henry was wrong, the look on Miss Feather's face told him everything he had said was true: Nathan would never see his mother again. He'd never have the chance to say good-bye, to tell her he loved her. Because she was gone.

She was gone forever.

And at that moment Nathan realized that nothing in his life would ever be the same again. . . .

CHAPTER TWO

ONE YEAR LATER . . .

No one saw the mailman arrive.

It was too early; the sun wasn't due to rise for another hour when he cycled into the courtyard of the Tarside project. Even the two Tarside hobos, Turps and Charlie, hadn't woken yet. They were still snoring soundly in their spot in the corner of the parking lot, behind the burning Dumpster that had been burning now for twenty-three consecutive days. A record.

No one saw the mailman arrive that morning because all three tower blocks of the project were slated to be demolished within the month and everyone with any

CONTENTS

The Moving Finger writes; and, having writ,
Moves on; nor all your Piety nor Wit
Shall lure it back to cancel half a Line,
Nor all your Tears wash out a Word of it.

—Omar Khayyam

Time flies like the wind.
Fruit flies like bananas.

—Groucho Marx

CHAPTER ONE

THE BUS

When Nathan's father told him the news, his voice seemed lost in the quiet of the schoolroom—*as though it didn't belong,* Nathan thought.

Nathan couldn't remember his father, Henry, having ever visited the school before. Not for parents' evenings, or school plays. Not even when he and Nathan's mom were still married. That's why when Nathan saw Henry's car arrive at the school gates, he knew something terrible had happened. By the time his teacher, Miss Feather, called Nathan into the school office, Henry was already waiting for him, his face as gray and crumpled as his tie.

"Nathan, it's your mother," Henry began. "She's been in an accident."

Henry waited for Nathan to say something, but Nathan was silent. He couldn't speak. His mouth was dry, and he felt a numbing ache against his forehead, as though a cold fist were pressing down on him.

"She was hit by a bus," Henry continued. "The driver didn't see her until it was too late."

Nathan hesitated. "But she's okay?"

"No, Nathan. No. I'm afraid she's not."

The fist pressed down harder, and Nathan felt hot tears prick his eyes. It had been only a few hours since he'd last seen her. As he was leaving for school, she'd kissed him once on the cheek; then she'd pulled on her coat—the green one Henry had bought her for her birthday. She was leaving too, and so they walked out of the house together. The last thing his mom had said to him was not to come home too late because they had plans for the evening.

"But we're going out tonight," Nathan told Henry, remembering. "We're going to see a movie. We'd planned it," he added, trying to make Henry understand—Henry knew how much Nathan's mom loved the movies.

Miss Feather was standing with Nathan. When he began to cry, she took hold of his hand, trying to comfort him, but Nathan didn't want her holding his hand. He didn't want her, and he didn't want Henry. He wanted his mother.

"We're going to the movies—*tonight!*" he told them.

"Nathan. Your mom's dead, son," Henry said, grabbing Nathan's arm. "Do you understand? She's gone."

"No—she's not! She can't be!"

He couldn't believe she was dead. He didn't *want* to believe it. He didn't want to think that he'd never see her again. Never hug her, or—

"It's a mistake," he said. "It has to be a mistake."

"I'm afraid it's no mistake, Nathan. She's dead. I'm . . . I'm sorry."

Nathan shook his head. But no matter how much he wanted to believe Henry was wrong, the look on Miss Feather's face told him everything he had said was true: Nathan would never see his mother again. He'd never have the chance to say good-bye, to tell her he loved her. Because she was gone.

She was gone forever.

And at that moment Nathan realized that nothing in his life would ever be the same again. . . .

CHAPTER TWO
ONE YEAR LATER . . .

No one saw the mailman arrive.

It was too early; the sun wasn't due to rise for another hour when he cycled into the courtyard of the Tarside project. Even the two Tarside hobos, Turps and Charlie, hadn't woken yet. They were still snoring soundly in their spot in the corner of the parking lot, behind the burning Dumpster that had been burning now for twenty-three consecutive days. A record.

No one saw the mailman arrive that morning because all three tower blocks of the project were slated to be demolished within the month and everyone with any sense had long since moved out.

Everyone, that is, except the residents of one apartment on the thirteenth floor of Tarside Heights: Henry Cobbe and his son, Nathan. They were still asleep when the mailman's bicycle rattled to a stop beside the vast crane that had been delivered in the night to demolish the first of the towers. They didn't hear the mailman humming "Ring of Fire" to keep his spirits up, nor his voice echo against the red wrecking ball that hung down from the crane like a great steel jawbreaker.

No one heard it—except Marbles.

The mailman opened his bag and paused, thinking he heard something growl in the shadows. He listened to the wind in the tarps hanging from the towers above. Each was the size of a basketball court, with the word CONDEMNED written in black paint. They clapped in the night, like a ship's sails.

The mailman glanced at the crane; he glanced at the shadows in the corner of the lot. He shrugged.

"Just the wind," he told himself, and he pulled a bundle of envelopes from his bag. They were addressed to Henry Cobbe of Apartment 134 Tarside Heights. They had been lost in transit for weeks, some of them for months. Every one of them should have been delivered by now, but each morning something had managed to stop the mailman: an accident in the road, the chain of his brand-new bike snapping, his shoes catching fire. Always something inexplicable.

But today he was determined that the mail would be delivered. It was the only reason for him to be here this morning, the only reason for anyone to be here. There were no other residents of the Tarside project.

Only Henry Cobbe and his son.

And Marbles.

"Hello?" the mailman said, hearing something rumble in the shadows behind the Dumpster. Two black eyes shone at him like firecrackers in the dark. "M-marbles, is that you?"

Marbles shuffled, blinking, into the light. He was Turps's pet gray-faced pug, and despite being no bigger than a microwave oven, he was mean—a bundle of fur and teeth and hate, and not necessarily in that order.

The mailman didn't need a second warning. He scrambled his shiny new fireproof shoes onto the pedals of his bike and set off for the nearest tower. His new chain made a satisfying whizzing sound as he passed the burning Dumpster—but he knew nothing could outrun Marbles. Even before the mailman's bike had reached the shelter of the crane, the little terror was snapping at his mudguard.

There was a great *pop* as Marbles's jagged teeth bit into the back tire. The bike was out of control. It barreled on to the first tower and smashed right into the wall. No one heard the sound of tearing trousers, the gnashing of teeth. And no one saw the bundle of letters addressed to Henry Cobbe explode into the air and scatter on the wind. No one heard the mailman's cries.

No one saw and no one heard.

It was too early.

Or, perhaps, it was too late.

Cronos.

He was one of the Titans—the Greek gods of the Earth and the sky—and apparently kind of a fruitcake.

At least that's what Nathan thought. After all, if Nathan was to believe his father, Cronos ate his children, fearing they would rise against him in the future and crush him. That's pretty crazy for starters. Never mind what he did with the sickle. Of course, these being the Greeks, that wasn't the end of the story. Later, his sixth child, a geezer called Zeus who had avoided being eaten by Cronos, made his old dad drink a potion that caused him to vomit up his five children, and they escaped.

Nathan's father had taught him all this before breakfast. Henry was bit of a worrier. He worried so much that he suffered from stomach ulcers and had to chew special pills the doctor gave him. He worried so much that his hair was falling out. Nathan never knew what Henry found to worry so much about—maybe it was his job or the shabby state of his car. Maybe it was the fact that the building in which he and Nathan lived was going to be demolished in a month and he hadn't found a new home for them yet.

Maybe it was all these things. Nathan didn't know exactly.

But he *did* know what worried Henry most at the moment was the fact that the thick, black hair that was disappearing from the crown of his rather squareish head would never grow back. Ever. And that made it fall out even faster. It was a vicious circle.

". . . he gets mixed up a lot with Chronos with an 'h.' *He's* the personification of time," Henry said. "But Cronos *without* an 'h' doesn't really have anything to do with time. He just ate his kids, that's all."

Outside it was still dark, and Henry glanced out of the kitchen window and down at the parking lot, where a crumpled bicycle lay near to the burning Dumpster, its rear wheel revolving solemnly in the orange light of the streetlamp. "Looks like Marbles has bagged himself another mailman," he said, turning back to the counter. As he buttered his toast and poured a second cup of black coffee, he burped and explained how Cronos's worrying was all for nothing anyway. "Zeus and the other children came back and crushed their dad, and they sent him to suffer terrible torments in hell," he said glumly. He stared at the coffeepot as though he had a lot of worrying to do and not enough time to do it.

"Actually," he said, "it wasn't really hell. It was a place called Tartarus, in the underworld. A little like the Underground at rush hour," he added. When he realized what he'd said, he glanced up quickly to see that Nathan wasn't about to burst into tears.

"N-not that everyone who dies goes to hell, Nathan," he said. "Your mother. I'm sure, well, if anyone deserved to go to heaven, she did—"

"I know, Henry," Nathan said, getting up and grabbing his bag.

Henry picked up his car keys from the counter.

"And don't forget—you've got Mr. Hernandez's class after school."

"Yes, Henry."

That had been almost eight hours ago.

Eight hours, thought Nathan, but it was still the most interesting thing he'd learned all day. School had been like poor Henry's hair—it had gone nowhere fast. The morning had started off ominously—double-period French with old Mr. Scattergoods. While the class conjugated verbs, Nathan pulled out his blue notebook. He had begun doodling Cronos tearing his kids to bits in his teeth when Moll, who sat next to him, looked over his shoulder.

"What's that?" she asked.

Nathan told her what Henry had said about Cronos, about how he ate his kids and threw them up and was sent to hell.

"So your dad's still nuts?" asked Moll, who liked to call a spade a shovel.

"Kind of, yeah."

"Cool." Moll shrugged. She looked at the drawing. "Needs more blood," she said.

Before the bell rang for morning break, Nathan had pretty much mastered the black, fathomless O of Cronos's mouth and the sharp zigzag of Cronos's teeth. During lunch break he'd drawn Cronos's children being eaten—or what was left of them. And while lovely Miss Feather was describing European crop rotation in the fourteenth century, he had scribbled black menace into Cronos's deep-set eyes, and red blood onto the thick fingers of his clawlike hand.

"If you could go back in time, where would you go?" Moll asked, while lovely Miss Feather told them about the lovely spinning jenny.

Nathan shrugged. "I'd rewind back to this morning and not bother getting up," he said. "What about you?"

"I don't know," replied Moll, mulling it over. "I'd go back and invent the internal combustion engine."

Nathan paused and gave Moll a dubious glance. "But it's already been invented," he said.

"Well," Moll said, unperturbed, "so someone must have gotten there before me." She looked over his shoulder. "Needs more blood," she added.

By the time the school bell rang at the end of the day, Nathan had added a few scattered stars in the background and a pile of bleached bones by Cronos's feet.

"Too much blood," said Moll, when they were standing together at the school gates. "Blood—that's a sign of an agitated mind, you know, Nathan." She winked. "See you Monday, okay?"

"Monday?"

"Yeah, it's Friday today—it's the weekend, you numpty."

"Yeah. See you, Moll," said Nathan.

He watched Moll turn down the street, joining the other kids. Everyone was headed home, back to civilization and TV. Everyone, that is, except Nathan. Nathan didn't head home. As the streetlights blinked on above Moll's head, burning like phosphorescent bars of pink soap, Nathan turned and headed for the community college on New Cross Hill, and to Mr. Hernandez's physics review class. It was where Nathan had spent the evenings of the last couple of weeks, and where, if he did what his dad wanted, he would spend each subsequent evening until the Christmas holidays started, one month from now.

Nathan had been sitting quietly in Mr. Hernandez's class for about an hour, when he pulled out his blue notebook and stared at the picture of Cronos. As he looked at it, he began to notice that the anxious expression he'd doodled in Cronos's eyes was a little like his father's. The bald spot and the hunched shoulders and crooked front tooth were his father's too: his father, Henry Cobbe.

Dad—he'll be driving over to pick me up soon, Nathan thought brightly. He looked up at the clock above Mr. Hernandez's desk.

The clock said it was two-thirty.

That can't be right, Nathan thought, and he checked his watch. Then he remembered that whatever the time, the clock above Mr. Hernandez's desk always said it was two-thirty. In fact, for all Nathan knew, it never really *was* two-thirty in Mr. Hernandez's room. Certainly he'd never seen it, because he'd only ever been here in the evening. *Every evening for the past two weeks,* he told himself, looking at his watch. But it too had stopped.

And I'll be here every evening till the holidays, he thought, winding it. By then, he knew, Mr. Hernandez's physics review lessons would be of no use at all. *By then, nothing will be of any use,* he thought, *because I'll fail the exams anyway, and my life will be over.*

Almost before it had begun.

That's what his dad, Henry, had told him, so it had to be true. After all, Henry Cobbe knew about failure. He was an expert.

It was this particularly dismal future that was occupying his thoughts when Nathan saw the Beefeater pass by the open door.

CHAPTER THREE

THE LONESOME YEOMAN OF NEW CROSS HILL

There are moments in one's life when one cannot believe one's own eyes; when the world of dream and reality move so close as to be indistinguishable—usually an hour before dinnertime. This was just such a moment for Nathan. But he knew there was no chance that he had imagined it. *He* had been there just now, walking down the hall. As large as life. A Beefeater.

Nathan didn't know a great deal about Beefeaters, and what he did know he'd learned on a school trip to the Tower of London. He knew their correct name was yeomen warders. He knew they wore black-and-scarlet uniforms with big, brimmed hats. He knew they carried pikes and were supposed to guard the crown jewels.

And he knew one of them was in New Cross Hill Community College tonight.

If it had been any other evening, Nathan would have simply ignored the lonesome Beefeater. After all, it wasn't so strange for a Beefeater to be roaming the hallways of New Cross Hill Community College, was it? *Some of them must have a yearning to learn to speak Esperanto, mustn't they?* he thought. Or master the arts of ceramic glazes? Or the Peruvian nose flute? Or flower arranging? *And if they didn't, then their wives might,* Nathan thought.

But this was not any other evening. This was the evening after the evening before, when Nathan was sure he had seen the exact same Beefeater wander down the exact same hallway at the exact same time. So when Mr. Hernandez's digital watch beeped for the end of class, Nathan picked up his things and dashed into the hall before Mr. Hernandez had time to stop him.

He followed the direction the Beefeater had gone. He was burning with curiosity. Henry was always late these days, so Nathan knew he would have plenty of time to see what the Beefeater was up to.

The college was a grim sort of place at night—the kind of place where Nathan thought he might at any time come upon the scene of a crime. The fluorescent lights buzzed like a toothache, and Nathan imagined their dim light catching the shape of a corpse spread-eagled on the floor. He looked at the fly-spotted walls and imagined a pool of seeping blood, or a bag spilling counterfeit money across the cracked linoleum.

Nathan wondered if this was the reason the Beefeater was here; maybe he had chased a felon all the way from the Tower of London, his ceremonial pike cutting a path through the evening crowds.

It wasn't likely. The Beefeater was a big man, but he was out of shape, and what Nathan had seen of him suggested he was barely capable of running a knitting competition at a retirement home, let alone hunting down a violent criminal across half of London.

He was *tall though,* thought Nathan as he peered through the safety glass of the various classroom doors that lined the hall. *Very nearly a giant.* He tried the handle of the nearest door. *Almost seven feet—*

Nathan stopped. His train of thought had been momentarily derailed by the peculiar sight that welcomed him from behind the door: There, in the teachers' lounge of New Cross Hill Community College, the giant—and rather portly—Beefeater knelt before an armchair in which an elderly man was sleeping. He was holding the untied laces of the sleeping gentleman's Hush Puppies between his fingers. As the ribbon of light from the hallway crept up to the Beefeater's face, he turned and glanced at Nathan and—rather coolly—raised a finger to his lips.

"Shhh!" he seemed to say.

Nathan stepped back out to the hallway and closed the door. He took a moment, then opened it again to make sure he had not imagined it.

He hadn't.

The enormous Beefeater was still kneeling in the same spot, his finger still pressed to his lips. He was apparently unabashed by his discovery. In fact he looked strangely proud, and the more Nathan looked at him, the more Nathan felt he was somehow intruding on a private moment.

"Sorry," he said, blushing. And he began to back away ever so slowly, as though the Beefeater were a bomb that might go off without warning. Nathan closed the door and sat himself down on a chair in the hallway. He barely looked up as the college's perky-looking cleaning lady whizzed by atop her Nelson Turbo floor polisher—she performed a neat figure eight on the linoleum before buzzing away down the hall like a drunken bee.

Nathan was baffled. *Maybe the pressures of the exams have taken their toll,* he thought. *Maybe I've lost my mind. It happens,* he thought. He'd seen programs on TV about it: kids going completely loopy. Scientists had tested it under laboratory conditions.

"The human brain can cram in only so much before it

bursts at the seams like an old vacuum bag," the man on TV had said, pointing vaguely at two plump guinea pigs sitting in a cage, "flinging equations and equilateral triangles and ratios around like so much pink custard."

It was a scientific fact: Too much learning could discombobulate a person.

Maybe that's what's happening to me, thought Nathan. *I'm being discombobulated!* This particular thought, however attractive, didn't last long, because Nathan knew he didn't really care about exams. That was the problem. They just didn't register in his mind. And that was exactly why he would fail them.

No, it wasn't the exams that had gotten to him. It was Henry.

Or rather, Nathan thought, *it's Mom.*

It was a year to the day since Nathan's mother had died. *Has it only been a year?* he thought. It seemed so long since he'd last seen her that he had begun to fear he could no longer remember what she looked like. He could only remember clearly the smile on her photo, which Henry kept on the mantelpiece. It had become a false memory—fixed in time.

Her name was Cornelle, and she and Henry had divorced years before the accident. Henry had been living alone in an apartment in Peckham. Nathan had hardly seen him since the divorce, but after his mom died, it was decided that Nathan should move in with Henry.

It was a big change for them both. It wasn't that Nathan didn't like Henry. He did. In fact he adored him. And Henry was doing his best—Nathan knew that. But Henry's best was, well, not very good. That's why Nathan's mom had left him in the first place.

But he's gotten worse, Nathan told himself.

Since his mom had died, everything had pretty much gone to pieces. Everything, including Henry.

Henry—

Darn, Nathan thought, getting to his feet. His dad would be waiting outside, in the car. He glanced at his watch. It said . . . two-thirty!

He still hadn't moved when the door to the teachers' lounge opened and the giant Beefeater stepped out, an expression of childlike joy in his placid eyes. Dressed in his black-and-scarlet uniform, he really did look like a giant from a storybook. His buttons shone like Christmas lights. As he closed the door of the teachers' lounge behind him and joined Nathan in the corridor, Nathan glimpsed the old gentleman inside—he was still sleeping soundly.

The Beefeater winked.

"Mum's the *word,* Nathan," he said.

CHAPTER FOUR
THE BOY WHOSE MOTHER DIED

"Now, what's next?" the Beefeater asked, fumbling in the pockets of his tunic for something.

"What?" Nathan said, confused.

"Our next task," the Beefeater said, addressing Nathan as though he were an accessory to a crime. "Oh, where is it?" he said. "I had it written down somewhere. Ah! Here we are!" He pulled a bus ticket from his pocket and held it up like a prize.

Nathan shrugged. He had no desire to spend any more time in an empty building with a man who read bus tickets for fun and untied strangers' shoes in the dark, so he said, "I've gotta go. My dad'll be waiting. By the way, you left your hat in there," he added, over his shoulder. "And your stick thingy."

"Pike," the Beefeater said.

"Gesundheit!"

The Beefeater went back inside. When he returned with his pike and hat, Nathan was halfway down the hall. "Your father, Nathan," the Beefeater said, in a voice that was both impossibly deep and soft, like distant drums. "I'm afraid he won't be arriving anytime soon."

Nathan stopped. "What?"

The Beefeater blinked his black, impassive eyes. He had found whatever he was looking for on the bus ticket, and he folded it neatly up and replaced it in his shirt. Then he paused for a moment, as though awaiting a signal. He stood beneath the flickering fluorescent ceiling light like an assassin caught in a lightning storm.

"What did you say?" Nathan repeated.

"Oh, nothing," the Beefeater said in his rumbling sort of voice, before setting off at a canter in the opposite direction.

Nathan stumbled after him. "You said my father won't be coming. What do you mean he isn't coming? Why isn't he coming?"

The Beefeater smiled. "Fathers are always late—they're completely unreliable. It's the law, isn't it? " he said enigmatically. "Anyhow, the traffic's terrible. Some snarl-up at the Embankment." He stroked his neat graying beard thoughtfully. "Is the school secretary's room this way?" he asked, pointing down a flight of stairs with one great blunt finger.

"Th-the . . ." Nathan stuttered. "I don't know," he said. Nathan felt that he didn't know anything anymore. "Look, I'm going now, okay?" he said.

"Of course," answered the Beefeater as he peered down the stairs. Then he started suddenly, as though an idea had struck him. "Oh—but I don't suppose you're the boy, are you?" he asked.

"What boy?" Nathan said as the lights above his head flickered a third time and then blinked off altogether. He jumped. Someone had turned off the power. The college building was closing for the night.

Nathan's heart seemed to stop as behind him the baritone voice of the Beefeater rang out from the blackness:

"The boy whose mother died!"

Nathan froze. He held his breath.

In the solid dark of the hall something stirred. A bright flash of light burst against his face, causing him to stumble backward, falling to the floor. He could do nothing but watch as a small disc of blue light, like a newly minted coin—like a firefly—danced in the darkness before casting itself against the Beefeater's huge face. The whole of the Beefeater's enormous head seemed to be floating in its light, disembodied.

"It's later than I thought," the Beefeater said. "Here—"

An enormous hand dragged Nathan to his feet.

"Sorry about that, Nathan," the Beefeater said. He was holding a flashlight in his hand, and he grimaced playfully toward it. "Word of advice: Always keep a flashlight handy, in case of emergencies," he said, struggling to shine its pale beam at the stairwell. "Now, follow me," he said.

"Wait! How do you know my name?" Nathan asked.

"What?"

"You said my name," Nathan said without moving.

"No I didn't," said the Beefeater as he hopped down the stairs.

"But . . ." Nathan bit his lip and followed the Beefeater's lead. He found a main switch on the ground floor and turned it on. As the light returned, Nathan realized that the Beefeater's sharp, black eyes were aimed directly at him. They were not wholly friendly eyes, but Nathan had to admit that they weren't wholly unfriendly, either. *Merely mischievous*, thought Nathan. Like a boy with a secret. Still, set as they were in the gray driftwood complexion of the Beefeater's face, they formed an unpleasant contradiction.

"My mother," Nathan began in a small, measured voice. "She died a year ago."

The Beefeater nodded like a man who had just been told his dry cleaning wouldn't be ready until tomorrow.

"You said you were looking for a boy whose mother had died," Nathan added. "I suppose it might be me."

The Beefeater scratched his beard.

Nathan gave up. "Oh, forget it," he said, and he turned and walked toward the exit.

"Wait!" the Beefeater called. He rushed past Nathan to a short passageway and to a bright red safety door. "Look. The secretary's office," he said, beaming. He opened the door and went inside.

"Congratulations." Nathan sighed.

He was ready to leave the Beefeater to his own sinister devices when he heard a lot of rattling and banging coming from the office. He looked inside. The Beefeater was throwing open the drawers of the large gray filing cabinet and pulling out all the files, tossing them down on the secretary's desk.

"Hey, you can't do that," Nathan cried.

"What?" murmured the Beefeater, without looking up from what he was doing. "Oh, are you still here? We were wondering whether you were the boy, weren't we? Well, let's see," he said, sitting himself in the secretary's chair and opening a number of files. He was clearly enjoying himself.

"There are a few questions that need to be asked," he said. "First—*are* you a boy?" He glanced at Nathan. "Indeed, you do seem to be a boy. Secondly, are you present here in the New Cross Hill Community College tonight, the nineteenth of November?" He glanced a second time at Nathan. "Yes, you are. Good job!"

Nathan watched as the Beefeater took the contents of one file and placed them in a second file. He did the same to the next two files, and to eight more. Then he moved on to the envelopes the secretary had set aside to mail the following day.

"Now," the Beefeater said, switching the enclosed letters from one envelope to the next. "Has your mother died recently?" he continued. "The answer is yes. Is your father dead? Yes. Is the—"

"Wait," interrupted Nathan. "My father's alive. I told you, he's waiting for me outside, in his car. Right now."

The Beefeater met Nathan's words with a look of profound pity. "Oh dear. Bad luck then," he said. "Alive? That's too bad." He shook his head. "Then I'm afraid it can't be you. The boy I'm supposed to meet here is an orphan." He smiled sympathetically. "Oh, but while you're here, would you mind making yourself useful and keep a lookout?" he said. "I hate to be disturbed while I'm at work."

Nathan watched as the Beefeater switched the contents of each of the remaining envelopes and sealed them again. He wondered who the Beefeater was and what exactly he was doing here.

"You're from TV, aren't you?" Nathan asked, getting an

idea. "One of those reality shows." He glanced up at the secretary's shelves to see if he could spot the hidden cameras. "That's it, isn't it? It's all a gag for a TV show."

"Do I look like I'm *from TV*?" the Beefeater said without stopping.

"No. You look like a giant Beefeater."

"Exactly."

"So, where are you from, then?"

"Chadwell Heath," the Beefeater said, standing up. He stepped across to a large bulletin board that was hanging on the wall. On the board were small color photos of each member of the teaching staff, about a dozen in all. With a little excited skip, the Beefeater switched the names under all the photos until every photo was labeled incorrectly.

"But—but why are you untying old men's laces and mixing up files?" Nathan asked. "It's just, well—*mean,* isn't it?"

"Nonsense," the Beefeater replied. "Where would we be if all our documents were filed correctly?" he said, and he picked up a big blue eraser and began to erase the phone numbers in the secretary's address book. "Have you ever thought what would happen if no mistakes ever occurred?" he asked, grabbing a pen and replacing the erased numbers with new—random—numbers. "Children would never smile," he continued. "People might never meet and fall in love. Why, you might not even be here, Nathan, you might never have been born."

"That's ridiculous."

"Is it?"

"Yes," concluded Nathan.

"Ah, *but is it*?" asked the Beefeater, with a superior twinkle in his eye.

"Yes."

"Well suit yourself. Only, consider this," said the Beefeater. "Imagine that when that sleeping man in the teachers' lounge wakes up—let's call him Godfrey Pooter of 29 Acacia Avenue, just for interest's sake. Well, say old Godfrey stumbles out of the room and trips over his untied laces, falling into the arms of the cleaning lady, whom he has admired from afar for three years without having told her. Let's call her, oh . . . Enid Pidgin. And imagine that when Enid and Godfrey meet, they fall in love. Doesn't that justify a small act of foolishness?"

Nathan shook his head. "No. You can't go about ruining people's work, and . . . and untying their shoes," he said.

"I can," replied the Beefeater, grinning. "I do."

"But you can't!"

The Beefeater looked steadily at the boy. He seemed rather startled. "No, perhaps you're right," he answered, rising. He swatted forlornly at a little calendar on the desk. "Maybe it is all nonsense," he said, "all of it. And I'm a fool." The Beefeater looked crestfallen. "What with chaos spreading throughout space and time, and the world about to come to an end," he added. He was so disheartened that he could manage only the slightest of smiles as he pushed the calendar off the desk and into the wastepaper basket.

"The world is coming to an end?" repeated Nathan.

"Is that what I said? Oh, don't you listen to me, I'm just having one of those days."

The Beefeater frowned. Then in a flash the dark mood that had descended upon him seemed suddenly to vanish. His eyes began to twinkle once more, and in an instant he looked like a man who had never entertained a negative thought in his life. He was *laughing*.

"You're nuts, aren't you?" Nathan said, nervously.

"What?"

"Nuts, a nutcase," Nathan said. "Bonkers, a loony tune, got a screw loose, a sandwich short of a picnic, mad as a bag of frogs," Nathan said. "You're nuts."

"Yes. Yes, of course," said the Beefeater. "That's it. Of course, yes. I'm a lunatic. You've seen right through me, Nathan."

"There, you said it again!"

"Said what?"

"You called me Nathan!"

"Did I?" the Beefeater said. "Perhaps I did. . . ." He rolled his black eyes. They were so black that Nathan thought he could see his own reflection flash in them.

The Beefeater gave him a sly smile. "Well, Nathan, you've figured me out, haven't you?" he said. "Never mind. You go and find your father. Go home. Forget you ever saw me."

Nathan flinched from the Beefeater's smile. "Thanks. I will," he said, stepping back to the safety of the hallway.

"Unless . . . "

Nathan stopped. "Unless?" he said.

The Beefeater's head appeared around the side of the door. "Unless you *are* the boy I was talking about," he said. "This orphan boy. But of course, you can't be, can you?" he added sarcastically. "Your father's alive and well and waiting outside in his little car, isn't he? Well then, good-bye," he said. The Beefeater waved his large, square hand.

Nathan walked to the exit, but as he pushed open the doors, he heard the great man's voice echo down the corridor:

"But if you do bump into the boy, tell him I'm looking for him, will you, Nathan? . . . My name is *Bartleby*!"

CHAPTER FIVE

PEANUTS

Once he was outside and standing alone under the somber streetlights of the Queen's Road, Nathan had the absurd fear that the Beefeater was still behind him. He hesitated to turn around in case the giant bearded head of the yeoman warder was floating there at his shoulder, like a huge jack-o'-lantern, leering at him.

But the Queen's Road was mercifully free of disembodied heads. And jack-o'-lanterns. And once Nathan had walked around the block, searching the night for the shape of his dad's gray Ford Escort, he was pretty sure it was free of Henry Cobbe, too.

Nathan looked at his watch.

It was two-thirty.

"Of course it is," Nathan said. If he hadn't been so unnerved, he could have laughed at the joke of it all. The Beefeater, the clock, now his watch—they all seemed cracked. But as a red double-decker Routemaster bus rumbled to a standstill at the bus stop opposite, a small doubt crept into his thoughts. What was it the Beefeater had said? A snarl-up at the Embankment? *And Henry isn't the calmest driver in the world, is he?* thought Nathan. *And the Embankment, that's where Mom was hit by a bus, wasn't it?*

Maybe the Beefeater was right. Maybe something terrible had happened.

No, he told himself, *it's just Henry being Henry again.* But what if there *had* been an accident? He should get home and wait by the phone. Just in case. That would be the sensible thing to do, he told himself as the bus revved its engines.

The bus—

"Wait!" Nathan shouted. With one hand he tried to catch the bus driver's attention, and with the other he pulled off his shoe and grabbed at the change he had hidden in his sock—Henry had let him down a lot lately, and Nathan had started keeping some money in the bottom of his sock for this very eventuality.

"Wait!" he called, waving the sock in the air. He had almost reached the opposite sidewalk when a single starry light shone in the road. For a moment his mind turned to the Beefeater and his flashlight. He froze, waiting for the Beefeater's great, ghostly head to appear. But rather than a flashlight rising up over the slope as he'd imagined, there appeared only a headlight, and rather than a Beefeater's floating head, there came a shabby-looking gray Escort. Henry's Escort. And Nathan remembered that the left headlight of Henry's car had burned out a week ago and his father couldn't afford to replace it.

"You're late," Nathan said as the car pulled up beside him.

Henry pushed open the passenger door. The car smelled of starched towels and liquid soap. A dozen yellow antiseptic mothballs rolled around on the floor, like so many sour-smelling bird eggs. "I said, you're late."

Henry steered sharply into the path of the bus, causing the driver to brake. The bus's horn blared.

"Death traps, those red Routemaster buses," Henry grumbled. "I don't care what you say, Nathan. The best thing they ever did was decide to get rid of them!" His wedding ring tapped against the steering wheel in time with "Ring of Fire," which was playing on the radio.

For some reason it hadn't struck Nathan as odd that it was a Routemaster standing at the stop. He wondered what it had been doing there, now that the Routemasters had been decommissioned. *Perhaps it's a tour bus,* he thought.

"Mom liked them, Henry," he said. And it was true—she had liked them. "Besides, it wasn't the bus's fault," he added. "Mom—it was raining, the driver, he . . . " He stopped. He could tell that Henry wasn't listening.

"Was it the Embankment?" Nathan asked, after a medley of country-and-western songs had finished. They were almost in Peckham now, the silhouette of Tarside Heights rearing up above the rooftops like a savage box of cereal.

"Was what the Embankment?"

"Why you were late," said Nathan.

"Put your sock on," said his father, stroking his hand across his bald spot.

"It's not my sock. It's one of yours. I couldn't find mine this morning."

"Then put *my* sock on," Henry said.

"Can't yet."

"No such word as *can't*, Nathan."

"Yes there is. It's in the dictionary."

"Not in *my* dictionary, Nathan. Anyway, what's happened at the Embankment?" Henry asked, watching out of the corner of his eye as Nathan struggled with his shoe.

"Oh, just something I heard," Nathan said.

Henry parked the Escort in their spot by the garbage cans, and he and Nathan walked up to the steps of Tarside Heights, ignoring the burning Dumpster that had been aflame now for nearly twenty-four consecutive days. A record.

Nathan looked up at the crane with its wrecking ball. It loomed against the sky like a monster, looking down upon the two Tarside hobos, Charlie and Turps, who were playing cards in the corner of the lot. Charlie was wearing a paper pirate's hat. He waved it as Nathan went by, and Nathan waved back. Then he stopped, seeing Marbles scurry out from underneath a fallen tarp. The old pug started furiously toward Nathan and Henry. He was almost upon them when Nathan pulled a stick of chewing gum from his pocket and tossed it in the air. Marbles caught it with a sharp *snap* of his jaws and began to chew contentedly. It was a trick Turps had taught Nathan: Chewing gum was the only thing that could curb Marbles's temper, apparently. Bubble-Lite. Pineapple flavor.

"Don't encourage him," Henry said as Marbles set about blowing a pink bubble that was as large as his head. Henry ushered Nathan inside.

"Dad, what do you know about Beefeaters?" Nathan asked as the doors to the elevator opened. They were almost up to the thirteenth floor before Henry answered.

"Waste of money, Nathan. That's what I know about Beefeaters," he said.

He unlocked the door of their apartment and walked

straight down the hall and into the kitchen. He turned the kettle on. "Have I told you that your grandfather was a Beefeater? Grandpa Cobbe."

"Yes, Henry."

Nathan had never known his grandfather Cobbe. He had died when Nathan was a baby. Henry never talked about him. All Nathan knew about him was that he'd worked as a Beefeater for a while, and that he was a loser.

"He was a loser, Nathan," continued Henry. "He wasted his life doing that dumb job, and he got paid peanuts."

"If Beefeaters get paid peanuts, then how is it a waste of money?" Nathan asked.

Henry pursed his lips. "It's a fact, Nathan, they're just there for gullible American tourists to take photos of, son. Like those red buses," he said.

"Are there any *giant* Beefeaters?" asked Nathan.

Henry thought about it. "I don't know, son," he said, "but I do know they're a giant waste of money. Standing around the Tower guarding a bunch of crows that are never gonna go anyplace anyway. Just in case."

"In case of what?" Nathan said, yawning. The clock in the kitchen had stopped, but he figured it was almost seven now. He sat down and turned on the TV. Henry went to start the shower as the kettle boiled.

"Well," Henry said, calling from the bathroom, "according to *them*, if those mangy old crows fly away, then the

Tower of London will crumble or the world will end—or something," Henry said, turning on the hot water. He caught himself in the mirror above the toilet and puffed out his chest, admiring his profile. "Course, what the American tourists don't know is that the crows can't fly away because they've had their wings clipped," he said. "They're going nowhere, Nathan. No, your Beefeaters have got it easy, son. They should try selling soap for a living—*that* would fix them."

Soap was Henry's favorite subject, because that's what Henry did: He sold soap. He sold it to hotels and factories. Soap and toothpaste and things like that. And according to him it was the hardest job in the world. Rocket science had nothing on selling soap, he always said. "You can't wash your hair with a rocket, can you?" he'd once told Nathan. And Nathan had to agree. *But it doesn't explain why Henry is so set on me passing my physics exams,* he thought.

"Another bad day?" Nathan asked.

Henry didn't answer. He only blinked at his reflection in the mirror. On the TV the newscaster was saying a new sort of mule had been discovered in Borneo that could speak Esperanto. Henry made himself a cup of tea. He was about to tell Nathan that it was all nonsense, and that Esperanto wasn't a real language anyway, when he noticed that Nathan was curled up fast asleep on the couch.

"Future's not what it used to be, Cornelle," Henry said,

glancing at the framed photo of his former wife—Nathan's mother—that was set on the mantelpiece. "No, you're better off where you are," he added, shaking his head. "Only wish I could be with you, sweetheart."

There was a dry lump in his throat as he took another sip of his tea. Then, making sure Nathan was still asleep, he kissed the corner of the frame and went to take a shower.

Nathan blinked his eyes open.

He didn't know how long he'd been asleep, but on the TV some pink-haired woman in Chipping Sodbury was saying that her beloved Chihuahua had driven off in the car and performed a perfect U-turn in the road. She was very proud, yes, she said.

The clock on the VCR said two-thirty.

"Henry?" called Nathan. There was the smell of burned toast coming from the kitchen, and on the TV a report had just come in from Sweden about a man who had turned Norwegian in the night.

Nathan got up from the couch. He noticed that the door to the bathroom was ajar.

"Henry, you in there?" he said.

The apartment was silent except for the dreary drip of a faucet.

Nathan pressed his face to the bathroom door. He hesitated. When Nathan was nine, he and his dad had gone for a swim in the local pool and Nathan had accidentally seen his dad naked in the changing rooms. He never wanted to repeat that horror again, so he called Henry's name once more and counted to ten before peering inside.

Despite the thick brown steam the room was freezing cold, and when Nathan stepped inside, he felt the hair on the back of his neck stand up in alarm: The shower was empty. His father was nowhere to be seen.

"Dad?" Nathan gasped, and he began to shiver. There was a draft coming in through the bathroom window. Nathan turned around to close it, only to see that there *was* no window. It had disappeared. There was no longer a window, and there was barely a wall. There was only the bright night sky facing him through a hole in the plaster and the brick: a clot of silver stars that shone from a man-sized smash in the side of the apartment—a Henry Cobbe-shaped hole.

"Dad?" Nathan uttered.

He took a step toward the hole and looked down at the ground far below, half expecting to catch the figure of his father falling in slow motion through the air, toward the parked car and burning Dumpster.

But there was no figure, and no man falling. There was nothing but the hole.

Henry was gone.

CHAPTER SIX
THE MANTRA OF HENRY COBBE

Nathan sat back down on the couch. He was cold, and his head was aching. He wondered why he wasn't crying, or why at the very least he wasn't upset. After all, his father was gone. Blasted somehow through the bathroom wall. Dead, for all he knew. Yet Nathan wasn't even shaking.

It wasn't like when his mother had died.

Nathan remembered how he'd heard the news that she'd been in an accident. He was in class—it was history, with Miss Feather. It had snowed that afternoon and Nathan had been staring out of the window at the wet puddles and daydreaming as lovely Miss Feather described what ghastly thing Henry VIII had done to one of his lovely wives.

That's when he saw Henry's car.

And that's when he knew it was serious. Serious enough for Nathan to be let out early from class. Serious enough for Miss Feather to walk him to the school office.

He remembered watching Henry's face as Henry told him about the accident on the Embankment. How the bus driver hadn't seen Nathan's mom step into the road. And he remembered how his face never flickered once. It was as if Henry were describing a brand-spanking-new shampoo to a hotel manager, or a new, zesty-fresh toilet cleaner to the owner of a nursing home. Henry had been thoroughly professional about the whole thing—until Nathan began to cry.

Crying was something Henry Cobbe couldn't handle—crying and hair loss and making toast without burning it. As soon as the first tear had squeezed itself from Nathan's little face, Henry wilted, folded in on himself, crumpled like a house of cards.

They'd driven over to Henry's apartment at Tarside in silence. Once inside, Henry had sat Nathan down on the couch.

"Time for a cup of tea?" he had said, excusing himself from the living room as Nathan sobbed alone in front of the TV. It was *Who Wants to Be a Millionaire?*

Nathan had known at that moment that he would never

get over his mother's death, not really. And of course he hadn't gotten over it, and neither had Henry. But Nathan pretended they had, for Henry's sake. Because that's what Henry Cobbe wanted most in his life: to get over things. Don't let yourself dwell on it, was Henry's advice. Pull yourself together and get on with things.

The mantra of Mr. Henry Cobbe.

Nathan felt a guilty pang as he watched the spangle of distant traffic through the Henry-shaped hole in the bathroom wall.

I should do something, he thought. But what? He wondered whether he should call the police. But he'd seen enough TV to know they weren't interested until twenty-four hours had elapsed. And besides, what would he tell them? That his dad had been blasted through two feet of concrete?

And then it came to him.

As the kettle boiled, he switched off the TV and turned out the lights. Then he was back in the bathroom, standing before the hole with a cup of tea in his hand.

He placed the cup against the shaving mirror. The hot tea caused the glass to fog, and in the condensation he wrote BYE, before walking out of the room and out of the apartment, shutting the door behind him.

Outside, things were different too.

Nathan noticed that the record-breaking Dumpster had finally burned itself out. Turps and Charlie's card game was done, and they had left. Charlie's paper pirate hat was lying flattened on the concrete.

Everything, it seemed, was peaceful and quiet. Nathan had never known Tarside to be so quiet. He didn't like it. There was no sound of bottles being broken or fireworks being set off. No car alarms were screaming out; there were no police sirens. There was only the hum of traffic passing on the road across the way, and somewhere a radio was playing "Ring of Fire." There was nothing at all to suggest that a worried, balding middle-aged man had been sucked out of his bathroom by unseen forces—not even a few pieces of concrete on the ground.

Nathan looked up at the apartment building. He thought he could see the smash in the bathroom wall on the thirteenth floor. It looked like a man silhouetted against the light—a father waving to his son, perhaps. Nathan felt a bit foolish waving back, but as he did so, a peculiar notion came to him: He realized he was an orphan.

And he remembered what the Beefeater had said.

No. *It was a just a coincidence,* he told himself. *There are thousands of nutters in London, aren't there? It just so happened that I met one on the same day my dad was blown through the wall.*

Could happen to anyone, he told himself, and he started walking toward the High Street.

He stopped at the intersection, an empty feeling in his stomach, and he turned in time to see a bright red Routemaster bus pull up beside him. Nathan glanced idly at the windows of the bus, and for a moment he thought he saw the Beefeater's black-and-scarlet uniform through the glass.

Nathan shook his head. *Great. Now I'm seeing things as well,* he thought. He was looking at his watch before he remembered that he already knew the time:

Two-thirty. It had been two-thirty all day.

Nathan felt very alone. He was about to go look for a police officer when his eye was caught by a scarlet shadow on the top deck of the bus as it pulled away.

There was no doubt about it now. He hadn't imagined it.

It was the Beefeater, Bartleby.

He was on the bus!

CHAPTER SEVEN
THE 230 TO THE EMBANKMENT

Perhaps it was the sudden realization that he was alone in the world, or perhaps Nathan's mind had finally snapped, but seeing the Beefeater, Nathan felt his hopes inexplicably soar. He began to run for the bus. If it hadn't been for a gray car cutting in front of it, Nathan might never have caught up at all. But as the bus's horn shrieked out, he leaped for the rail and fell in a heap on the platform at the bottom of the steps.

"Tickets?" asked the round, unaccountably cheerful bus conductor; he waited as Nathan pulled off his shoe and sock and counted out his change.

"Thanks," Nathan said, when he was handed his ticket.

Then he ran up the stairs.

There, in the trash in the aisle of the top deck, he could see the enormous heels of a pair of black, shining boots peeking out from under the seats. And an enormous rear end.

"Blast!" came a voice.

"H-hello?" Nathan said, creeping forward.

There was a short silence, then: "Fiddlesticks!"

Nathan saw the hands of the Beefeater flash in the shadows, snatching up the used tickets that had been thrown to the floor.

"Bartleby?" called Nathan. There was a *clang* as the giant Beefeater stood up, banging his head on the ceiling.

"Oh, it's you," he said, rubbing the back of his skull. "What is it? Your father late again?"

"Something like that," answered Nathan. "What are you looking for?"

"A bus ticket," Bartleby said. He sat down and began to smooth out a dozen or more tickets that he'd picked up from the floor.

"Didn't you buy one when you got on?"

The Beefeater frowned. His black gaze was distracted and fleeting. "No. Yes. I mean, it's a particular ticket, Nathan. I had it earlier. It had a reminder note scribbled on it," he said, discarding three tickets. Then four more. Soon he had no tickets left, and he just sat there shaking his head.

"Is it important, this ticket?"

"I'd say it is."

"Why, what's on it?"

"Oh, something about mending the fabric of Time—"

"Do you always write notes on bus tickets?"

Bartleby lifted up his great face. "Why should a man buy notepaper when he's already paid through the nose for a bus ticket?" he replied. "That's simply a waste of a good ticket."

"You sound like my dad," Nathan said. The bus's horn blared out again, and Nathan looked out of the window and was astonished to see they were traveling over Blackfriars Bridge. "What bus is this?" he asked.

"The two-thirty to the Embankment," replied Bartleby. "Here—I don't suppose you have a ticket, do you?" he asked.

"A ticket? Yes, of course I do," Nathan said. He was staring at the Thames shining like silver in the night, wondering how the bus could have gotten there so fast. *Peckham to Blackfriars,* he thought. *That's at least three miles as the crow—*

He stopped and watched a large black raven fly past the window, as though conjured from the air by his very thoughts.

"Let me see it," Bartleby said.

Nathan handed him his ticket.

The Beefeater's face lit up.

"Why, this is it!" he bellowed. "Where did you find it? Oh, never mind, as long as I have it. Now at last we can get on with things."

"Get on with things?" Nathan asked, turning away from the window and the river.

"Of course. Finding this boy," Bartleby said. He was literally bouncing with enthusiasm, like a big—rather sinister—puppy, and the bus began to groan under his tremendous weight. It rocked from side to side.

"Oh, but that's what I wanted to tell you," Nathan said, starting to feel a little giddy. "This boy, you see," he said. "It's me. My dad, he's disappeared. Gone. Through the wall."

"Through the wall, you say?" The giant Beefeater grinned. "Fascinating. But what has that to do with me?"

"Don't you see? I'm an orphan now," Nathan explained. The word *orphan* seemed bitter on his lips, and he felt his eyes begin to sting. "I'm the boy you were looking for at the college, remember?" he said.

Bartleby had stopped bouncing now. He was listening to Nathan in rapt silence.

"Mmm," he said when Nathan was done. He stood up. "This is my stop," he said. But he thought twice about reaching for the bell; instead he regarded Nathan's face fondly. "I'm sorry, Nathan," he said, "but you can't be the boy I'm looking for."

"I can't? Why can't I?" Nathan's head was swimming, and there was fear—an awful fear growing now in the pit of his stomach. He was beginning to see the reality of the situation. He could see what the next few days would be like. The police would come and see him; they'd ask him about his father. And there'd be journalists. All of them would want to know what he'd done with Henry. Because people didn't just blast through walls, did they?

And if Henry didn't come back, then what? Social services? A children's home?

"I'm sorry," Bartleby said, his eyes shining sadly. "But you see, written on this ticket is the name of the one person who might set the world right—save it from destruction. And that isn't a task to be trifled with, is it?"

"No," Nathan said. He shook his head. "But is the world really in danger?"

"*This* one is, certainly," Bartleby answered. He glanced through the window to the night sky. "It has already begun, or haven't you noticed?" he said. "Time is out of kilter."

Aside from the fact that it always seemed to be two-thirty, and that his dad had been shot through the bathroom wall, Nathan thought things were fairly normal. *An average sort of day*, he thought sarcastically. He looked up at the stars.

"Do you think what happened to my dad might have

had something to do with this kilter thing?" he asked.

The Beefeater smiled. "Who knows?"

"You'll miss your stop," said Nathan, struggling with a smile of his own.

Bartleby pressed the bell, and a look of great sorrow fixed in his eyes. "Oh, see here," he said, stopping at the stairs. "Just to make sure," he said, and he straightened out the ticket Nathan had given him. He read the note on the back. "Your name, Nathan," he said. "It isn't Harvey Rodeo, is it?"

Nathan grinned. "No, Bartleby," he said. "No. My name's Nathan. Nathan Cobbe."

"That's a shame," Bartleby said. "I think you might have done just as good a job." He grabbed for the rail as the bus came to a shuddering stop and missed, dropping the ticket. When he picked it up again, his eyes flashed like beacons. "Wait," he said, reading it again. "Blast it all, I'm a fool, Nathan. I was reading it upside down." He laughed. "Look, what did you say your name was?"

"Nathan Cobbe," said Nathan.

"Nathan Cobbe. That's it! That's the name!" roared the Beefeater. "Now, hurry up, Nathan, this is where we get off!"

"Are you sure?" Nathan said, rushing to his feet and following Bartleby down the stairs.

"Look for yourself," said the Beefeater as they jumped

off the bus. He handed him the ticket. Nathan held the bus ticket in his hand and read the name scrawled on the back. It read:

NATHAN COBB

"It's spelled wrong," Nathan said.

The bus had dropped them at the sidewalk beneath an imposing row of buildings.

The night was dark, and there was a chill in the air; it smelled of snow.

"Oh, it's the traditional spelling," Bartleby said. "Your father always did have ideas above his station. He thinks the extra 'e' makes it look grand." He smiled wanly. "But Henry always was a twit!"

CHAPTER EIGHT

BANG!

Nathan frowned. “How do you know so much about my dad?”

Bartleby’s black gaze slid silently across Nathan’s face.

“I don’t. But I know twits, Nathan,” he said, “and your Henry’s a twit.”

“No he isn’t, he’s just . . .”

“A twit?”

“Worried.”

“Worried that he’s a twit?”

Nathan shook his head. “Worried about everything! Henry, he’s . . . he’s had a lot of things on his mind. Since Mom died—”

Bartleby clicked his tongue. "Since your mom died, your father's been living in the *past,*" he said coldly, and he glanced at the sky and then at the road.

"You don't understand," Nathan said.

Bartleby stepped down from the sidewalk and started across the street.

"I understand more than you think, Nathan. Here, this way," he said, without waiting for Nathan to follow. A mail truck came down the road, and Nathan paused to let it pass before rushing after him. In the distance he could see traffic crawling bumper to bumper. There were pedestrians, too, all of them huddled against the cold and the *snow*.

"It's snowing," Nathan gasped. He watched the ghostly flakes spin on the breeze above his head. They fluttered like moths against the streetlights. *It didn't even look like snow earlier,* he thought. And he shoved his hands in his pockets to keep them warm.

"It'll pass," said Bartleby.

They moved on toward the lines of traffic. The sidewalks were bustling with people running to escape the snowfall, and Nathan had to fight to keep upright. Only when they had been walking for a minute or more did he glance up to see where they were headed. The road was wide and busy, and he could see the river beyond the heads of the passersby. There was something familiar about the place, but the bus journey had so disoriented him that he could have been anywhere—the Houses of Parliament or Greenwich dock.

Then he saw the lights.

There were Christmas lights strung out across the road, hanging from the streetlights and fizzing and flashing against the bruised gray clouds.

"I didn't think they were turning on the lights till tomorrow," he said, under his breath. He shivered against the cold lap of the snow and sleet and turned to Bartleby. "Where are we?"

Bartleby paused. "You mean, '*When* are we?' "

Nathan slipped on the wet sidewalk. "What?" he said, grabbing hold of Bartleby's arm to steady himself. Bartleby held his wrist firmly and began to lead him through the crowds. "The time, Nathan," he said. "What time is it?"

Nathan hardly needed to look at his watch. "Two-thirty," he gasped, trying to catch his breath. He hadn't noticed the sky brightening, nor the sun peeping from between the clouds. He hadn't noticed it was no longer nighttime.

"Good, we're right on the dot," chimed Bartleby.

"On the dot for what?" Nathan asked, as a man in a wet gray suit bumped into him. He was knocked sideways and lost his grip on Bartleby's arm. For a moment the glare of the headlights from the traffic blinded him, and he imagined he saw the back of the man's squareish balding head as he ran on, disappearing into the crowds.

All at once Bartleby was beside him, pulling him up. "To show you what kind of man your father is," he said.

"Henry?" Nathan said, finding his feet.

The man with the squareish head had vanished.

"What do you mean?" Nathan said. "What kind of man is he? What's all this about?" He glared at Bartleby's face—straight into his black eyes. "Who are you?" he asked.

The Beefeater stared back at him. "That's an awful lot of questions, Nathan," he said implacably. "Which do you want me to answer first?"

Nathan didn't like the Beefeater's tone, nor the dark turn the night had taken. Or rather, *the light turn,* he thought, correcting himself. Indeed, glancing out at the road, he saw that the snow was clearing now, and so was the sky; the clouds had begun to break. A bright drizzle was falling. *In fact, it's much too light to be night,* he thought. The clouds were impossibly clear and bright, and small darts of sunlight had begun to pierce the gloom.

In this supernatural setting the Beefeater appeared to Nathan as some abominable genie. He even smiled smugly, like a genie who had tricked Nathan into making two wishes and knew he had only one remaining.

Nathan swallowed hard. "All right," he said, deciding on his question, "tell me this: Are you really a Beefeater?"

Bartleby smiled quietly to himself. He knocked the melting snow from his sleeve with a casual sweep of his hand. "I *was* a Beefeater, Nathan, in the past," he said. "Now I'm . . . well, it's hard to explain what I am now."

"If you're not a Beefeater, then why do you pretend to be one?"

"Because I like the uniform." Bartleby smiled. "Black and scarlet's terribly slimming, don't you think?"

Nathan looked at the great figure of the Beefeater. Slimming *isn't the first word that comes to mind,* he thought.

"If you're not a Beefeater, what is it you do?" he asked as they continued their way down the road. At every other step Nathan noticed a shape of the skyline that he recognized. A spire or dome, or tower. They caught his eye because they were all lit in that same twilight shade as the streets. They gleamed in the drizzle as though they had been painted.

"Right now, Nathan," Bartleby said, "what I do is save the world from your dad."

Nathan stopped. He wasn't sure whether he'd heard him right.

"My dad? Henry?"

"Yes." Bartleby nodded. "Mr. Henry Cobbe of Apartment 134 Tarside Heights, Peckham—with an 'e.' Your father, Nathan. He's destroying it right this minute, or he will if we don't stop him."

Nathan couldn't believe what he was hearing. He couldn't believe any of it—the snow, the crowds, the daylight breaking through the clouds. "You're wrong," Nathan argued. "Dad can't destroy anything. He wouldn't!"

"Why wouldn't he?"

"Because . . . because," said Nathan, struggling to remember something important. "Because he's *dead*," he said at last. "He blasted through a wall, remember?"

Somewhere in the road a car horn sounded.

Bartleby shrugged. "Oh, there's probably a perfectly reasonable explanation for it," he said. "Perhaps he stepped out for a pack of cigarettes. You hear about it all the time on TV."

"He doesn't smoke."

"Some milk then."

"He's lactose intolerant."

"Then he went to get some air."

Nathan couldn't contain himself. "What? Through a wall?"

Bartleby only smiled. "He may have been desperate," he said.

Bartleby had a way of talking that made everything Nathan said sound silly, and everything he said sound perfectly normal. It was as though he lived by a different sort of logic from everyone else in the world. And yet Nathan couldn't help but think that maybe the Beefeater was right, and that it was everyone else who was wrong.

"Sometimes men destroy things without ever meaning to, Nathan," Bartleby said, seeing Nathan's confusion. "I'm not saying Henry wants to do anything wrong, only he is, without knowing it."

They were causing a holdup on the sidewalk, and Bartleby pulled Nathan into a doorway, out of the way of the pushing and shoving of the crowd. In the distance Nathan could see a figure in a green coat. The image struck him because it seemed familiar. There was something familiar about everything here, and he was reminded of his mother, Cornelle. Then he saw the man in the suit again; he was running.

"But what I don't understand—" Nathan started. He had barely opened his mouth when there was a loud *bang* from the direction the man had been heading in. It was a hollow, metallic sound that shook the sidewalk, and shook the crowd. It was like the sound before a dead silence. Then someone screamed.

"What was that?" Nathan asked. But he wasn't altogether sure whether he wanted to know the answer. An inexplicable fear had sprung up in his chest and taken hold of his heart, making it hard to breathe.

Finally, he recognized where they were: It was the Embankment.

Up ahead car horns screamed out. There was a commotion of some sort. Nathan could see people running to a spot in the center of the road. There, standing in the heart of it all, was a red Routemaster bus. It was stuck at an angle as though it had stopped suddenly.

"Bartleby!" Nathan yelled, grabbing hold of the Beefeater's arm. "What *was* it?"

Bartleby hadn't turned the whole time, he hadn't flinched. It was as though he had expected the whole thing: the *bang*, the horns, the raised voices.

"The beginning, Nathan," he said, quiet and calm. He glanced at the clouds above their heads. "Look," he said.

Nathan could see—above the streetlights, above the Christmas decorations, above the strings of gleaming bulbs and flashing neon—he could see that a great seam of green light was shining, like fool's gold, in the dark of the clouds. It looked like a smile—a horrible green smile.

"That . . . that's . . ." he began, fighting to get out the words.

"That's Henry's doing." Bartleby nodded. "The time is out of kilter."

Looking at the green smile, Nathan felt something swell in his chest. It felt like . . . terror.

"Come on," Bartleby said, guiding him away from the road. The sidewalk was emptying now as the crowd made its way to the incident in the road. Somewhere a siren wailed, and once Bartleby and Nathan arrived at the entrance of the Underground station, the air was ragged with the flashing lights of police cars and the ambulances.

Nathan braved one final glance at the Embankment. Then he shut his eyes and followed Bartleby into the darkness.

CHAPTER NINE

BARTLEBY EXPLAINS

The Beefeater breezed down into the Underground station, dashing between the turnstiles and turning down corridors. Nathan followed him without looking up. He was caught in Bartleby's peculiar energy like a capsized boat caught in the wake of an ocean liner.

"But if it's already started . . ." Nathan began, trying to make sense of the terrible scene on the Embankment. "If Henry . . . if it's happened, this kilter thing, then how can we stop it?"

"*We* can't, Nathan," Bartleby replied as they arrived on the platform. "*You* can!"

The platform was still and quiet, and Bartleby's voice

echoed from the close, curved walls of the tunnels. Somewhere, far away, Nathan could hear the sleek lines rattling in the tunnels, and there was the stifling breath of the trains in the air. It was suffocating.

"What do you know about time, Nathan?" Bartleby asked.

Nathan tried to recall the few things he'd understood from Mr. Hernandez's classes.

"Time," he said, "it's curved, isn't it?"

The Beefeater nodded sagely. "Now, no doubt you'll have heard that time is a string or a cube or a star that's folded in on itself, but that's all poppycock, unfortunately, Nathan. Truth be told, if I explained to you the secret of time, your brain would in all likelihood explode."

Nathan shook his head. "At least try!" he growled.

Bartleby clenched his jaw. He turned his back to the platform as a number of people joined them in waiting for the train. "Well then," he said in a low whisper, "imagine the world is an orange."

"An orange?" echoed Nathan. "What kind of orange?"

Bartleby paused. "It doesn't matter what kind," he answered.

Nathan sighed. "Then why bring it up?"

"Listen," Bartleby said, in a level tone, "do you want me to explain or not?"

Nathan nodded.

"Good." Bartleby sighed. "Now," he continued in a quiet, patient voice, "imagine the world is an orange, any orange. And imagine that time is the skin. Now imagine that skin slowly being peeled away, round and round, in one delicate coil. That is what is happening, Nathan."

Nathan thought about that for a moment. He pictured the orange, the peel, and he pictured the green crack in the sky. "But the orange would still exist without its skin," he said.

"Yes, but it's much easier to juice, Nathan!" Bartleby cried with a newfound spirit. "Have you ever tried juicing an orange in its skin? It's not easy."

"And we have to stop the orange being peeled?" Nathan said, hardly believing he was having such a conversation.

"Splendid, Nathan," Bartleby said, delighted. "You're catching on."

Nathan shook his head. He realized he'd been shaking it a lot lately. "And if we don't?" he asked. "What happens then? How will all this end?"

Bartleby beamed. "With a *bang*!" he yelled, as the air crackled with the charge of the approaching train. There was an unpleasant rush of warm air, and the people waiting stirred themselves from their private thoughts and stepped closer to the edge of the platform. None of them appeared at all interested in the Beefeater and his friend.

The tunnel was consumed in the din of the train as it shot into the station. In a moment the cars had come to a halt beside them, and Nathan and Bartleby stepped inside.

Nathan watched the dark walls of the tunnels begin to fly by as the train pulled away.

"If the world is going crazy like you say it is, then wouldn't it be on TV?" he asked.

Bartleby fixed his black eyes on Nathan. "If anything could convince one that the world is truly coming to an end, Nathan, it is *TV*."

"But what I don't understand is, what's this got to do with Henry? How can Henry destroy time?"

Bartleby leaned in closer. "I told you, Nathan. Henry is living in the past. Some men live in the past; some men live in the future. Very few live in the present. But Henry has gone that one step further than other men, Nathan. He is *returning* to the past. You see, time is an illusion. It is just nature's way of making sure everything doesn't happen at once. Henry's grief has taken him back in time."

Nathan glanced at the Beefeater's fantastic clothes, the eccentric line of his profile, the curiously black eyes. "Nuts," he said.

"If," Bartleby began, after a moment's hesitation, "you are suggesting that my assertion that time is an illusion is nuts, then I'm afraid it is far from nuts, Nathan."

"But Henry can't be living in the past," Nathan argued.

"The past's the past!"

"To most men," answered Bartleby. "But not to Henry. Henry has set himself to change the past."

Nathan persisted. "But the past is the past!"

"So you keep saying."

"But it is!"

"Then if the past is the past, as you say, it no longer exists, does it?" Bartleby explained. "And if the past no longer exists, then why should you still miss your mother, Nathan? Why does Henry feel so sad over the death of his wife? According to you, Nathan, the future doesn't exist because it hasn't yet happened, and the past doesn't exist because it's gone. So that just leaves the present."

"What's wrong with that?" asked Nathan.

Bartleby threw his hands up in the air. "What's wrong with that, Nathan, is that as soon as we consider the present, it is already the past. That's the thing about time—it tends not to wait around for you to catch up."

Nathan had no reply to that; he simply stared vacantly down the subway car. "So in that case . . . nothing would really exist."

Bartleby leaned back in his seat. "I know which theory I would choose to live by," he said. "If I knew there was nothing, that nothing truly mattered, then I doubt I would get up in the morning."

Nathan looked at the faces of the other passengers on

the train. They had no idea of the bizarre conversation taking place within the car. *How could they know?* he thought.

Bartleby sighed. "The truth, Nathan, is we have to stop your father. He doesn't know the damage he is about to cause."

"But he's already done it, Bartleby," Nathan said. "Whatever it is! You said so. I saw it in the sky. The green smile, I saw it!"

"You *can* stop it, Nathan, if you go back to the past," Bartleby insisted, taking Nathan's hand in his. "Remember—the past is not the past. The past, the present, the future: it's all around us!"

There was a squeal of brakes as the train approached a station. The lights flickered.

Nathan could only stare silently at Bartleby's steady, black eyes. They appeared supernaturally calm as the train rocked from side to side. And kind. There was a kindness in his face that Nathan had not noticed before.

"How do you know all this, Bartleby?" he asked. "Who are you?"

Bartleby faced him with an unsettling expression. It was some time before he answered, and when he did, the words seemed to catch in his throat.

"Haven't you guessed?" he said. "Why, I'm . . ."

As Bartleby opened his mouth, a terrible squealing erupted down the tunnel. The lights flickered out and

Nathan could see sparks as bright and terrible as stars explode against the outside of the glass. There was a loud *crash,* and a burst of thick, hot air filled the car, so hot that Nathan found it hard to breathe. There was the smell of burning, and he could taste oil on his lips. Something was on fire.

The last he saw of Bartleby was the black O of his mouth.

He heard the Beefeater yell: " . . . *I'm your—*"

Then there was a flash.

Then nothing at all for the longest time . . .

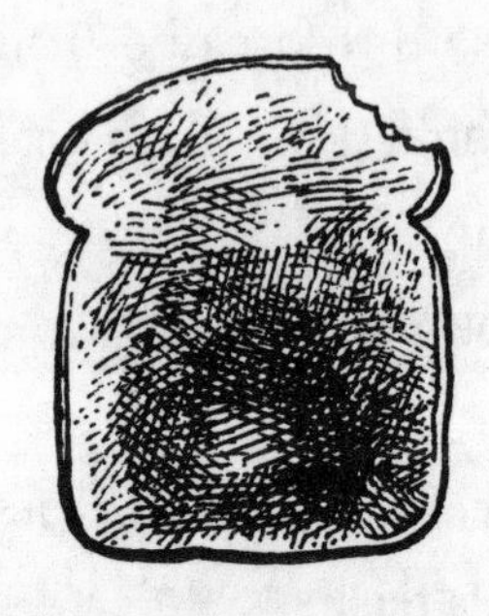

CHAPTER TEN
TO BEGIN AGAIN

Nathan stared at his cereal.

"... he gets mixed up a lot with Chronos with an 'h.' *He's* the personification of time," said Henry, who was warming to his subject. "But Cronos *without* an 'h' doesn't really have anything to do with time. He just ate his kids, that's all." He paused. "Looks like Marbles has bagged himself another mailman," he said, before continuing. "Anyway, it was all for nothing. Zeus and the other children came back and crushed their dad, and they sent him—"

Henry stood at the kitchen counter. He was holding a cup of black coffee in one hand, and with his other he was eating a slice of burned toast. He stopped, noting the peculiar way in which Nathan was staring at him. He put the hand holding the toast to his bald spot instinctively, and said, "What?"

Nathan stared back at the open blue notebook spread out on the table before him, at the bowl of cereal, at the spoon he was holding in his hand. A cold shiver ran up his spine, and the spoon fell into the bowl of cereal with a loud *plop*.

"Don't play with your food, Nathan," Henry said, sipping his coffee.

Nathan gaped at Henry. At the kitchen. The apartment. At Henry's toast. It was the same. Everything was the same. The train—it was gone!

It was all the same as . . . this morning.

This morning, or was it yesterday, or—

"Henry?" Nathan said, his wild eyes still fixed steadfastly on the bowl of cereal.

"Yes, son?"

"What's the date?"

"The nineteenth, I think," Henry said. He went to take a bite from the burned toast, and stopped. He eyed Nathan warily. "You all right, son?" he said. "Is the stress getting to you?"

"Stress?"

"From the exams."

"Exams?" muttered Nathan. "Um . . . no."

"If you don't feel well, you can miss Mr. Hernandez's class tonight, if you want. One night won't matter," Henry added with a smile.

Nathan was looking at Henry again. He knew he was staring, but he couldn't help it. He didn't know what had just happened. The Beefeater, the train, the Embankment—

"*What are you* staring *at*?" asked Henry. He put down the coffee and toast and moved to the exhaust-fan cover over the stove and looked at his reflection in the stainless steel. "There's not more hair falling out, is there?" he asked, his hand pawing gently at his bald spot.

"No," whispered Nathan. His eyes were drawn to the blank page in his notebook: The drawing of Cronos was gone.

"No," he said. "No, it's . . . *fine*."

"What's that?" asked Moll.

They were in Mr. Scattergoods's class. Nathan was at his desk, the blue notebook open before him. He was staring intently at the blank page, as though by staring he might somehow conjure up the doodle of Cronos. *Like I conjured the raven,* he thought. Maybe that's what all this was; maybe he'd conjured the Beefeater, too. Maybe he'd imagined it all.

But no, he knew the drawing had been there. He knew it had. He *had* drawn it.

"Um . . . what?" he said.

Moll frowned at him. "Did you tie your tie too tight again, Nathan? Cut off the blood supply to your head?"

Nathan wasn't listening—he was too lost in his thoughts, in the events of yesterday. Or was it today? He couldn't tell anymore.

"What do you know about Beefeaters?" he asked, when he eventually spoke.

"Beefeaters?" Moll chewed on the end of her pencil.

"Yeah."

School was the same, too. The trip from Tarside Heights, his father dropping him at the gates. Double French with Mr. Scattergoods.

The same.

"Well," began Moll, "they guard the Tower of London, don't they? And they get paid in beef. Honestly—I saw it on TV. Big slabs of beef. Why do you ask?"

Nathan picked up his pencil, and with a stumbling hand, he made a few faint lines on the page. "My grandfather was a Beefeater," he said.

The pencil scrawled the outline of an enormous figure, a pike and a hat.

"No wonder your dad always looks constipated," Moll said. "All that beef!"

Nathan continued the drawing of the Beefeater until the bell for lunch sounded. Then he went down to the cafeteria.

"But they're not magic, are they?" he asked, once he and

Moll were seated at their table and picking at their food.

"Beefeaters?" Moll said. "No. Only if you think big hefty guys wearing big flouncy skirts is magic. It's brave, but it's not magic."

Later, when lovely Miss Feather was going on about the spinning jenny, Nathan took up the conversation once more.

"If you could go back in time," he said, looking out through the window, to the space near the gates where his father had dropped him off that morning, "where would you go?"

Moll barely lifted her chin from the desk. "I'd invent the internal combustion eng—"

"No," interrupted Nathan, getting her attention with a flourish of the pencil. The Beefeater was almost finished now. The black, serious eyes, the beard. The buttons and buckles. "I mean, seriously, Moll. What would you do?"

Moll shifted in her seat. She considered the idea for a moment. "I'd stop my dad from leaving, the day he disappeared."

Nathan glanced at her. "Disappeared? *Your* dad disappeared?"

Moll's eyes met his briefly. They were warm and still. "Yeah," she said. "He was an overseas aid worker. He went abroad to check on a project two years ago, and he never came back. That's why I live with the Eckles, my foster parents."

Nathan didn't know Moll lived with foster parents. He knew nothing about Moll's dad or what had happened to him. Moll had never mentioned it before.

She shrugged. "They think he's dead," she said. "If I could go back in time, if it were possible, then I'd stop him from leaving that day."

Nathan stood at the school gates. Already it was getting dark. He could see the first of the streetlights blinking on, orange and dim in the distance, like candle flames. Moll appeared at his side.

"All right, Moll? You going home?"

Moll nodded. "How about you?"

Nathan looked at his shoes. "I've got physics review," he said. "Mr. Hernandez, at the college."

Moll said nothing. They stood together in silence, Nathan and Moll, as around them the other kids went their separate ways home.

"See ya, then," Moll said, finally.

"Yeah, see you later, Moll," said Nathan. He watched her go down the road, the lights blinking on above her head. Then he headed to the college.

All day his mind had been fixed on the matter of the Beefeater, Bartleby. He couldn't shake it. Every time he tried to think of something else, the fantastic shape of the Beefeater had risen up, blotting out anything that got in its way. Bartleby, and the idea that he had planted in Nathan's mind.

The idea that Henry could destroy the world.

It was ridiculous.

The whole thing was ridiculous: Bartleby, Henry, the hole in the bathroom wall. All of it. Absurd. Yet, it had happened.

The day had *repeated* itself. It was the same, exactly the same. He was sure. From the first minute until the last—*or at least until now*, Nathan thought, marching up the stairs of the college. And of course, if the day *was* repeating itself, he reasoned—if this *was* the same day—then the Beefeater would appear in the college at exactly the same time. And if he did appear in the college, then what? Wouldn't that prove it? That it wasn't all some dream, or a hallucination? Wouldn't it prove that what Bartleby was saying was true?

Nathan struggled to make sense of any of it. It was too much, too difficult. He couldn't even begin to fathom what it all meant. All he could do, he thought, was head to Mr. Hernandez's class. And if Bartleby appeared, then Nathan would confront him . . . and one way or another, he would find out what exactly was going on!

CHAPTER ELEVEN
THE COLLEGE

Nathan had to steel himself. He felt like his whole body was abuzz, seething with electricity. All through Mr. Hernandez's lesson he was on his guard, waiting for a glimpse of the Beefeater in the corridor, waiting to burst from his seat.

Waiting. Waiting.

But Bartleby didn't come.

Maybe he had missed him. Maybe he had looked away for a moment, just as Bartleby passed by. But he doubted it—he had hardly taken his eyes from the hallway the entire class.

Still, Bartleby wasn't there. He could be late. *Of course he could*, thought Nathan, trying to be optimistic. But when Mr. Hernandez's digital watch beeped for the end of the class, Nathan still hadn't seen any sign of the black-and-scarlet uniform.

"Nathan," Mr. Hernandez said as the class ended, "try to keep up in future, will you? Otherwise you'll never pass your exams. Here." He took a review form from his leather file.

But Nathan was already out the door and down the hall. Running. Frantic. Somehow he had missed the Beefeater, but he was determined to catch up. *He's here*, he thought. He must be!

The lights were flickering as Nathan reached the teachers' lounge door where, yesterday, he had first laid eyes on the imposing figure of the Beefeater. He swung open the door, expecting to come face-to-face with Bartleby.

But Bartleby was not there.

There was only the sad figure of Godfrey Pooter, slouched in his armchair. He snorted awake as the door clattered open.

"Hey, what's the joke?" he cried, fixing his pale, sleep-filled eyes on the figure in the doorway.

Nathan hesitated.

"I'm . . . sorry," he said at last, backing out to the hall and easing shut the door.

He looked briefly at the empty hallway, at the cracked

linoleum, the peeling paint on the wall, and the fluorescent lights. Then he made for the top of the stairs with the same uncontainable energy that had carried him to the teachers' lounge, desperate for any sign of the Beefeater.

He was running so fast that he very nearly ran into the cleaning lady, Enid Pidgin. She was at the top of the stairs, struggling to get her Nelson Turbo floor polisher to work. She gave it a kick as Nathan pulled to a halt.

"Enid, have you seen a Beefeater 'round here?" he asked in one breathless rush.

Enid Pidgin blinked. "Huh?" she said, without the first clue what he was talking about.

"Oh, never mind."

He leaped down the stairs and ran on toward the school secretary's office. Panic made him grab the handle; hope caused him to open the door and go inside.

He turned on the light.

Nothing. There was no Beefeater, no black and scarlet. No flashing buttons.

The filing cabinet was closed, the staff photos were all labeled correctly. The secretary's desk was neat and tidy. The calendar sat safely on the edge of the blotter.

Everything was as it should be, and yet everything was *wrong.*

It's wrong, Nathan told himself, as the lights flickered for the third time and then blinked out altogether.

He stood in the darkness, listening to the silence of the college at night. And finally he realized what made him wait here—why he didn't want to leave. This was all he had left: Bartleby and the night. Nathan couldn't accept that he had imagined it all, that Bartleby wasn't here, wasn't real. But how else could he explain it? No, whether he liked it or not, *something* had changed, and only he and Bartleby knew about it.

He stumbled his way to the college exit and went outside into the clear evening. He took in the road, and the bus stop opposite. He crossed over and sat down on the bench under the shelter. Some minutes later the bus arrived, as he knew it would. He knew because he had lived it all before. Every moment of it. *Nearly every moment,* he corrected himself.

Nathan stood up and walked to the end of the shelter.

He counted.

One.

Two.

Three.

Four.

On *five* a single headlight flashed above the crown of the road.

It was the Escort.

Henry pushed open the passenger door, and Nathan climbed inside without a word. The car smelled of starched towels and liquid soap. A dozen yellow antiseptic mothballs rolled across the floor, like so many sour-smelling Ping-Pong balls.

"Death traps, those red Routemaster buses," Henry grumbled as he steered into the path of the bus. Nathan didn't flinch when the horn blared. "I don't care what you say, Nathan," continued Henry. "The best thing they ever did was decide to get rid of them!"

He tapped his wedding ring against the steering wheel in time with the song playing on the radio. It was "Ring of Fire."

Nathan sat, silent, as they careened down to Tarside. He was silent as they parked in their space in the corner of the parking lot. After all, there was nothing to say.

He climbed out of the car and crossed the lot, glancing up only to take in the burning Dumpster that had been aflame now for twenty-five consecutive days. A record.

The crane and the wrecking ball loomed against the sky like a monster, looking down upon the two Tarside hobos, Charlie and Turps, who were playing cards in the corner of the lot. Charlie waved his pirate hat above his head as Nathan went by. Nathan waved back. As Marbles shuffled out from beneath the tarpaulin, Nathan reached for his Bubble-Lite chewing gum. Pineapple flavor. He threw a stick into Marbles's maw.

"Don't encourage him," Henry said, ushering Nathan

inside. Marbles blew a brief pink bubble in their direction and then returned to his tarpaulin.

"Henry," Nathan said, as the doors to the elevator opened. His voice sounded dry and hard. He cleared his throat. "Henry," he said, "what was Grandpa Cobb like?"

Henry looked steadily at Nathan. He was still staring when the elevator doors closed.

CHAPTER TWELVE

BEEFEATERS

They were almost up to the thirteenth floor before Henry spoke.

"Why do you ask?" he said.

"I just wondered," said Nathan. "You don't talk about him much."

Henry unlocked the door of the apartment, walked into the kitchen, and turned on the kettle. "There's a reason for that," he said, without volunteering more.

Nathan dropped his bag on the couch. "Wasn't he a Beefeater?"

"He died when you were little, Nathan. And he was a loser. He wasted his life doing that dumb job."

Henry untied his tie and held it distractedly in his hands. Without another word he walked into the bathroom and turned on the shower.

Nathan hesitated to follow. He didn't want Henry in the bathroom by himself. Even if the Beefeater hadn't appeared, there was still the chance that Henry might . . . might . . . In truth Nathan didn't know what he might do. *He may shower and then shave,* he thought. *He may even take a cup of tea in with him . . .*

Or he may be blown through the wall! whispered the nagging voice in the back of his mind. It was a deep, persistent voice. Like Bartleby's voice.

Nathan listened to the shower running. A moment later Henry returned from the bathroom.

"He got paid peanuts," he said, without looking up. "And when he died, he left your grandma in the lurch."

"Was he happy?"

"Happy?" said Henry. "I suppose so. He was lost in his own world, Nathan. Didn't have time for me or your grandma. If you don't have responsibilities, of course you can be happy," he added.

Nathan picked up the remote control and turned on the TV, trying his best to appear casual. Normal. "Perhaps he loved his job," he said.

Henry's mouth curled into a hard little shape. "Oh, he loved it all right," he said. "He loved the silly uniform, the routine. But the point is, he could have been anything, Nathan. That's the point. He could have achieved all sorts of things. Great things. But he wasted his time guarding crows."

"They're ravens, Dad."

Henry glanced up, his eyes a little wet. He seemed startled. He'd never heard Nathan call him "Dad" before. "He could have been a great man," he continued, pulling himself together, "but he chose to be a Beefeater."

"Perhaps he was a *great* Beefeater," persisted Nathan. But it was no use; Henry wasn't going to change his mind.

"That's why I made myself a promise," he said, gloomily. "I was your age. I promised that I'd make something of myself. A scientist or an inventor, perhaps. That I'd be a success, and rich." He shook his head ruefully. "Well, I haven't done a good job, have I?"

"You're the greatest soap seller in the metropolitan area," Nathan said, trying to cheer him up. "You're just in a slump, that's all."

Henry patted Nathan on the shoulder. "Thanks, son," he said, unconvinced.

Nathan could see some of the gloom lift in his father's eyes. "Did Mom like him?" he asked.

"Who?" asked Henry, as he poured the water from the kettle into a cup.

"Grandpa."

"Your mom liked everyone, Nathan. And everyone liked her."

Nathan sat down on the couch. He was pretending to watch TV, but in his mind he was trying desperately to pick the words that might make things right. "I miss her, Dad," he said, not daring to turn his face from the TV in case one brief glance might send Henry through the kitchen wall.

He heard his father sigh. Heard the *plop* of the teabag in the cup. He turned his head just enough to see, from the corner of his eye, Henry standing by the framed photo of Nathan's mom.

"So do I," Henry said.

There was an expression on his face that Nathan had never seen before. It was impossibly sad—and hollow. Like a man who had once held the secret to the world in his hand, but had since somehow mislaid it.

Nathan stood up from the couch. Beefeater or no Beefeater, he knew something was about to happen. It was all the same as before: Henry, the bathroom, the hole in the wall. It was all going to repeat itself.

He told himself that he wouldn't let his dad disappear, not again. He took a step toward the bathroom door. If he was going to prevent Henry from disappearing, Nathan knew that he had to stop him from going in.

"Dad?"

Henry took the tea in his hand and made for the door. Nathan lunged after him, but before he could stop him, Henry had walked inside and slammed the door shut.

"Dad!" Nathan grabbed the handle and yanked the door open.

Henry stood at the sink, sipping his tea. He blinked at Nathan, openmouthed.

"You want to use the toilet?" Henry said, nonplussed.

Nathan blushed. "Um . . . no," he stammered. He looked at the floor. Then, half turning, he glimpsed the TV screen. The man on the news was saying that a new species of mule had been found in Borneo that could speak Esperanto. . . .

Nathan closed the bathroom door.

He stood for a time looking at the narrow gap between the bottom of the door and the floor. He could see a little steam rise up from it and settle on the carpet like dew. He shook his head.

Stupid, he thought. Beefeaters? The world coming to an end? It was all stupid. All of it. And so was he. Some sort of dream, that's all it was. A dream.

Mom was dead—no more now than a vague, wonderful memory. And Henry? Henry was just Henry. That's all. No great mystery, no drama. Just one of those things. An accident. *And Grandpa Cobb*? Nathan thought. He was a loser, like Henry said.

On the TV the mule was counting to ten Mississippis. Nathan picked up the remote control. He had his finger on the OFF button when there was a loud *bang* from the bathroom. A bright white light flashed beneath the bottom of the door.

"Dad!"

Nathan was already through the door before the flash had died away. There was a great smash in the rear wall of the bathroom, and steam was billowing out into the night. A few dull stars sparked in the distance. The hole—it was Henry shaped!

Nathan planted his hands on either side of the broken brick and leaned out as far as he could, peering into the night. Henry was gone again.

Gone. Through the wall.

Nathan gasped. He knew he had to make a decision. He could either stay and wait for the police to come and take him away to prison or social services, or wherever—or he could go after his father; go after Henry and drag him back. He retreated a few steps and held his breath. *It's now or never,* he told himself. The orange peel, the great green smile. Now or never.

Before he could reconsider, he had launched himself toward the hole, and . . .

He jumped!

There was a flash, and a tremendous noise filled his

ears, as if the air had caught fire. Then silence. All around him was white; bright white light that shone against his face, as bright as the morning sun. It was like being trapped inside a lightbulb. *Or a Christmas light,* Nathan thought. And there was a smell, like the insides of a TV.

There was nothing to see and nothing to hear. There was nothing at all for the longest time.

CHAPTER THIRTEEN

THIS IS THE DAY . . .

It was afternoon on the Embankment.

Nathan gasped. There was a dull ache in his chest, as though he had been punched, and the air was cold in his lungs. It hurt to catch his breath. He looked up. The broad road of the Embankment was busy with traffic, and the car headlights shone against the falling snow. It whirled and spun in the air like dead leaves in moonlight. The sky was overcast and gray, but as the clouds rolled back, they broke at times with sunlight, and there were glimpses of blue at the edges of the storm.

Nathan shivered. He wasn't dressed for the weather. Rain was dripping from the Underground station roof and falling down his neck. He shuddered and took a step into the road, careful of the umbrellas of the passersby.

He stumbled a few steps, looking around, looking for something—but for what he didn't really know.

Perhaps Bartleby will show, he thought optimistically. He would have been glad to see anyone. *Even Mr. Hernandez would be good company,* he thought.

He was lost, bewildered, adrift in some strange place, some strange *time*. But what time?

The sidewalks were bustling with people running blind, trying to escape the snowfall, and Nathan had to fight to stay upright. He barely had a chance to admire the Christmas lights that were strung out across the road, that fizzed and flashed against the bruised clouds, before he was knocked off his feet by a passerby.

It was a man in a wet gray suit. Nathan climbed to his feet and staggered to the curb. For a moment the glare of the headlights from the traffic blinded him; then he imagined he saw the back of the man's squareish balding head as he ran on, disappearing into the crowds.

"Dad?" Nathan whispered.

There was no doubt about it. It was Henry, the Henry who had disappeared through the bathroom wall moments ago.

"Dad!" Nathan yelled, pushing past the crowd.

"Watch out," said one of the passersby.

"Careful," warned another.

"Mind yourself, kid!"

But Nathan was deaf to them. In the distance he could glimpse Henry's balding head bobbing in the crowd. He'd stopped to turn to face the road, as though he were expecting something to arrive. His face pale, haunted.

"Dad, wait!" Nathan yelled, but Henry didn't hear him. He was too busy trying to cross to the other side. The cars were bumper-to-bumper all the way down the Embankment, and as Nathan watched, Henry launched himself between them, running headlong into the road.

Horns blared. Brakes screamed. Drivers leaned out of their windows and yelled. But Henry didn't stop. He dashed across, skidding on the wet surface, his arms flailing, trying to keep his balance. He was running so fast now, Nathan knew he didn't have a hope of catching him.

But that didn't mean he didn't try. Taking his life in his hands, Nathan followed Henry across the road, through the traffic, past the blaring horns and irate drivers, out to the other side. He only just made it before a bus shuttled past behind him. It was a red Routemaster.

The appearance of the bus made him pause. There was something familiar, something chilling about the splash of red against the gray of the sky. A memory that he couldn't possibly own: the bus on the Embankment, the lash of the rain, the flash of Christmas lights. It was all familiar . . .

Mom.

A horrible realization came over him. *This is the day she died,* Nathan thought. The day on the Embankment. That's why Bartleby had brought him here. Then Nathan saw her, or rather he saw a figure in green some distance up the road. Without seeing her face or her smile, he knew it was her. She was standing on the curb, searching in her bag for something. Her hair was wet with the rain, and she was wearing the green coat with the fake fur collar that she liked so much, the one Henry had bought her for her birthday.

She was here—his mom, Cornelle.

And she was alive!

"Mom?" he called out, his voice cracking. He had staggered to a stop. He was too far away now, and too slow; he knew he would never catch up.

"Mom!" He lost sight of her as the bus moved into view. But he could still see Henry. He was maybe twenty feet away from her now. If only Cornelle had looked up, she would have seen him barreling down the sidewalk toward her. But she was too busy trying to pull her umbrella out of her bag. It was raining harder now, as the bus approached, and the sunlight was bouncing up from the puddles in the road and what was left of the snow.

Nathan saw it all. He saw the bus, and Henry, and his mother.

The bus had no time to stop. Besides, it was wet, and with the sunlight bouncing off the wet ground, the driver didn't stand a chance. It was only when Henry ran into the road that he braked. The bus's wheels skidded in the puddles.

Nathan saw Henry grab Cornelle in his arms, he saw the bus. He couldn't bear to watch. He knew neither had a chance of surviving. The bus was going too fast. As he pulled his hands up across his face, a great *bang* sounded that made his blood run cold: the sound of a collision.

Somewhere someone screamed. Then there was a blinding flash of light . . .

. . . then nothing for the longest time.

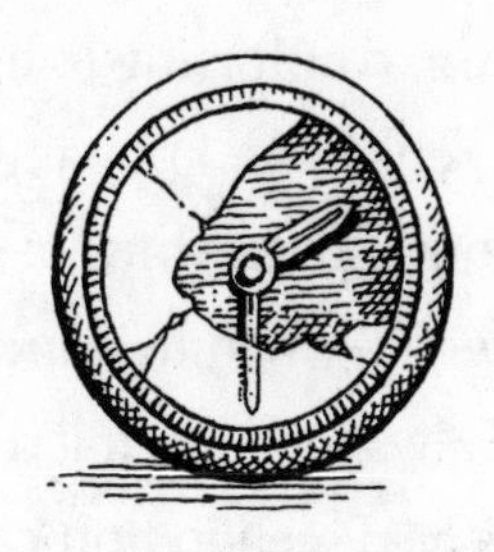

CHAPTER FOURTEEN

THE TV TIMES

"Nathan? *Nath-an?*"

A voice woke him from the light. *"Bad scratch you've got there, Nathan."*

It was a cheerful-sounding voice, a familiar voice, a man's voice, and it was accompanied by an array of cheerful-looking lights and the cheerful smell of antiseptic.

And there was piped music playing somewhere that was almost . . . *heavenly*!

At least, that's what Nathan thought. It sounded a bit like "Ring of Fire" played on a Peruvian nose flute.

He opened his eyes. For a moment everything was white and sparkly, and fresh, and he shivered as though he'd been caught outdoors naked. The last thing he could remember was being on the Underground train with Bartleby. He didn't remember going to the Embankment, but he remembered a *bang*. *The bang, of course,* he thought, seeing the pale, clean, comforting light. *I'm dead!*

It was a strange sensation, knowing you were dead. He didn't mind the lights and the smell of antiseptic. He didn't mind the cold. After all, when he'd imagined what heaven would be like, he'd always thought it'd be bright and clean, like the bathrooms he'd seen in home-improvement magazines. But he'd never imagined they'd have country music here.

Not in heaven. It wasn't . . . well . . . heavenly, was it?

And neither were physics teachers, he thought, staring dumbly across at Mr. Hernandez, who was seated opposite him, smiling.

"That's a bad scratch you've got there, Nathan," Mr. Hernandez said again, nodding cheerfully at Nathan's torn sleeve.

Nathan followed his gaze down and saw there was indeed a small spot of dried blood on his wrist, and he saw too that his watch was broken. The minute hand was still pointed steadfastly to half past, but the hour hand had disappeared altogether.

"Um, yeah," he said, his head still reeling. "Looks like it, doesn't it?"

"Funny stuff going on, isn't there?" Mr. Hernandez said, and only then did Nathan notice that his physics teacher was wearing a neck brace, and that his right arm was in a sling and his two front teeth were missing. He looked like he'd been wrestling with a particularly brutal equation, and the equation had won by a half nelson.

"Funny?" Nathan asked, blinking against the bright light.

"Funny, yes." Mr. Hernandez grinned. "This power-outage business. Half of London blacked out there for a few minutes. Did for me, Nathan, I can tell you. You try being bang in the middle of brushing Mars and Jupiter's teeth just when the blinking lights blink out. Believe me, Nathan, it's no fun. " He laughed.

"Mars and Jupiter?"

"My Rottweilers, Nathan," Mr. Hernandez said. "Mars and Jupiter. Great boys, but very sensitive. They hate the dark. With a passion, you might say!" He smiled a toothless little smile, as though to prove the point.

"Hmm," Nathan mumbled. He peered past Mr. Hernandez's unaccountably happy face to a long, pale hallway lined with chairs and stretchers. Dozens of bandaged people were being ushered into side rooms, and he could see doctors and nurses rushing here and there.

"This isn't heaven at all, is it?" he said, at last. "We're in the hospital."

"That's right, Nathan. Us and most of Camden, looks like. But everyone's coping. We're all in this together."

"Then I'm not dead?" Nathan muttered with a sudden bright realization, and he got up gingerly from the stretcher he'd been sitting on. Despite the blood on his sleeve, he was pleased to find that he was in no pain at all. He felt rather good—relieved, in fact.

"Dead? Certainly not." Mr. Hernandez chuckled."Wh-why should you think that?"

"There was a crash . . . the train . . ." Nathan said, struggling with his words.

"Train crash?" Mr. Hernandez laughed. "I don't think so, Nathan. If there'd been a train crash, I'd have heard about it. The news has been nonstop on the TV ever since I got here, see?" he said, nodding up to a TV set that was fixed to a wall bracket above Nathan's head. "Even canceled the horse racing for it," he grumbled, but in a cheerful sort of way.

Nathan looked at the screen.

It was true: The newscaster was saying how the whole power network had temporarily failed due to a family of Russian hamsters nesting in the Euston Road substation. There had been 140 reported incidents all across London, and scores of minor injuries, but thankfully, no fatalities—except for a particularly accident-prone hamster, he added solemnly, late of Euston Road.

Nathan watched as numerous accident scenes flashed up on the screen:

In Crouch End twenty-three senior citizens had been stuck down a manhole for an hour, passing the time by playing a game of Knock Down Ginger. In the Lambeth library there were fears that members of a school trip who had become pinned beneath the complete works of Shakespeare, large-print edition, were running out of oxygen. And a convention of football mascots had escaped from their hotel in Bethnal Green, and was believed to be on the run and heading for Wembley Stadium.

Then he saw a picture of the train on the Northern line.

"That's it. That's it!" he yelled, pointing.

Mr. Hernandez swiveled his glazed little eyes to the screen, taking a moment to focus. "He says it was just a breakdown on the tube," he said, repeating the newsman's commentary. "See, no crash."

"But I was there," Nathan called, turning from the screen to Mr. Hernandez's face and back again. There were other memories. Memories of Henry, and the apartment. Memories of the Embankment.

"I *was*," he said once more, but he was no longer so sure.

"Maybe you got a bump on the head, Nathan," Mr. Hernandez said. "Shock can do funny things to the noggin. Maybe you should wait until your dad comes back—"

"My dad?" Nathan said, turning from the TV screen.

"What about my dad?" he asked.

"What?" Mr. Hernandez asked, quite innocently.

Nathan stepped back as a stretcher carrying a rather flushed-looking man with his foot stuck in a toilet bowl was wheeled past.

"I said, what about my dad?" Nathan repeated.

Mr. Hernandez was still staring blankly at the TV screen.

"Have you seen him?"

The newscaster said there would be further updates on the London power outage later, but for now they were handing back to the highlights of the horse racing.

"Marvelous," Mr. Hernandez said. "Oh, yes, your dad, he should be back any minute now. Saw him five minutes ago, down there." He gestured to the far end of the hall—as best he could with a broken arm and a sprained neck, and no teeth.

"Oh, here," he added, struggling in his pocket to find some change. "If you're passing the coffee machine, get me a hot chocolate, will you? I'd go, only I'm not supposed to operate machinery, not until the painkillers wear off." He grinned.

"Of course," murmured Nathan, and he gazed across the heads of the crowd in the hallway, searching for any sign of his father.

He rounded the corner and found a woman in a nurse's uniform filling in a form on a clipboard. The badge on her lapel read NURSE SHEILA.

"Do you have a patient here?" Nathan asked. "His name's Henry Cobbe. With an 'e.' "

"Are you a relation?"

"He's my father." Nathan gulped.

"He's not dressed as Santa Claus, is he? Because I've had *him* in here tonight," she said, visibly flustered. It was clear she'd had a terrible day. "Easter bunny too," she added, annoyed. "And there's a couple of those football mascots giving me the runaround. When I get my hands on that pair . . ." She stopped, recognizing the sharp flame of anxiety in Nathan's eyes.

"Sorry, dear. Place is like a war zone tonight." She sighed, flashing a good-natured smile. "Do you know what he's here for, your father?"

"Not really," Nathan said, unsure of quite how he should explain that his father had been sucked out of his bathroom by a malevolent universal force that was as yet unidentified.

The nurse nodded. "I'll see what I can find out, dear," she said, setting off for the nurses' station. "Oh, and if you see two ten-foot chipmunks wandering about in football scarves, tell them Wembley's that way!" she said, pointing vaguely in the direction of the exit.

"Thanks a lot," Nathan called after her. He was surprised by how glad he was of the possibility that his father was here. That he was alive. He felt almost *happy*.

If only I could figure out what is happening to me, he thought—*what these dreams mean.*

As he made his way to the vending machine, he could still hear Mr. Hernandez's voice singing along to Johnny Cash over the hospital speakers, while on the TV, Onion Gravy was neck and neck with Jimmy Saville's Chin in the 2:30 at Chepstow.

He allowed himself a little smile.

"It wasn't real," he said, as he stood before the machine, pushing Mr. Hernandez's change into the slot. "None of it."

Some sort of hallucination, that's all, he reasoned, pressing the button. There was a mirror set in the front of the machine, and he peered at his reflection and saw that there was a small bruise forming at his temple.

"A bump on the head," he said, echoing what Mr. Hernandez had told him. "Shock can do strange things to the noggin. Make you see Beefeaters when there aren't any there. Make dads go blasting through solid walls. Make day night and night . . . *day.*"

A paper cup dropped out of the bottom of the machine with a *plop,* and an unpleasant shiver traced its way down Nathan's back.

Night and day.

A memory came back to him then, something awful scratching at a scab at the back of his memory: Christmas lights flashing against a gray, solemn sky. The sound of car horns. Snow on the Embankment. A head bobbing in the crowd—a rather square, rather balding head!

Before he had time to explore the memory further, another stretcher was wheeled down the corridor behind him, and in the mirror of the machine the reflection of a rather square, rather balding head slid past.

"*Dad*?" Nathan said, turning.

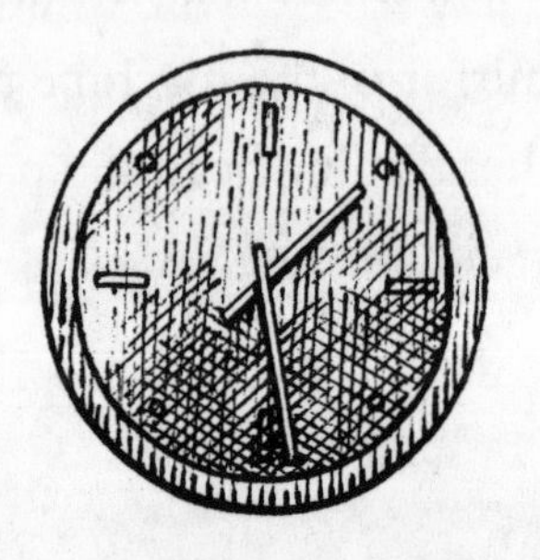

CHAPTER FIFTEEN
NOT THE END OF THE WORLD

"Dad?"

The stretcher continued down the hallway, a pair of yellow threadbare golfer's socks poking out beneath the blanket. Socks just like the ones Henry Cobbe with an "e" wore. The exact same make and style of sock as the ones Nathan was wearing this very minute. Henry Cobbe's socks!

"Dad!" he shouted, breaking into a sprint and grabbing the sleeves of the nurses who were busy guiding the stretcher into a side ward. He dragged them to a halt and stared down expectantly at the man laid out below, and was immediately disappointed.

An unfamiliar molelike man with a face like an unmade bed frowned back at him.

"H-hello?" the man said, blinking through a pair of thick spectacles. "Do I know you, son?" The man glanced at his wife, who was standing beside him, and shrugged quizzically.

Nathan sighed.

It was not Henry Cobbe, it was just another middle-aged man with thinning hair and dubious taste in socks.

"Sorry," Nathan whispered, "I didn't mean to . . . sorry." He sighed, heading back to the machine.

It wasn't Henry. *Course it wasn't,* Nathan thought, disheartened. Why would it be? His father was gone, shot through the wall of Tarside Heights. He'd seen the hole.

But then which one would you prefer? he asked himself, looking to his reflection in the machine and seeing the blue bruise continue to bloom. *That a Beefeater had come and told you your dad was going to destroy the world, before that self-same Beefeater was blown through the train window? Or that there had been a power outage and you'd hallucinated the whole thing?*

That Henry was here somewhere waiting for Nathan to come and find him.

Maybe he's had a knock on the head too. Maybe they had been in the train together: Henry and Nathan, during the blackout.

That's it, Nathan told himself. He and Henry had been

caught in the blackout, that's all. Nurse Sheila would find him in a moment and then they'd go home, back to Tarside Heights. No drama, no mystery—only a plain old blackout.

The hot chocolate frothed and wheezed, and finally the machine hiccupped to a stop.

Nathan picked up the cup and turned—

—and nearly spilled the contents of the cup over.

"*Moll*?"

"Nathan?"

Moll Timperley stood holding two bags of potato chips in her fist, looking from Nathan to the hallway behind her and back again, an expression of utter confusion on her face.

"Nathan?" she said. "What are you doing here? And what've you done to your head?" she added, peering at the scratch on Nathan's temple.

Nathan hesitated. "What? I'm—I . . ." he mumbled. "The blackout, Moll," he said finally.

If it were possible to nod sarcastically, Moll nodded sarcastically. "Yeah," she said. "I know about the blackout, Nathan. Everyone knows about the blackout! That's why we're here, remember? Are you feeling all right?"

"We?" Nathan began. "Well, no," he said, honestly. "No, not really. Feel a bit dizzy . . . Henry," he said. "I just thought I saw him, but it wasn't Henry. He was just wearing the same yellow socks as—"

Nathan pulled at one of his trouser legs to demonstrate, only to see that he wasn't wearing Henry's yellow socks. They were green. "Funny," he said.

"Henry?" Moll said. She looked doubtful and a little scared. Nathan had never seen Moll look scared before. He didn't think she was capable. "Maybe we should go look for a nurse," she said.

"Oh, I just saw one," replied Nathan. "She says she'll tell me when she finds him."

"Him?"

"Henry."

"Henry." Moll nodded. "O-*kay* . . ." She took Nathan's arm. "Look, I think we really should get back to Brian and Jan. They'll know what to do."

Nathan stood perfectly still. "Brian and Jan?"

Moll gripped his arm a little firmer. "Nathan, *really*, you are okay, aren't you?"

Nathan felt self-conscious all of a sudden. There were many strange things for his mind to contend with at the moment, and this particularly strange conversation was one extra strange thing he would rather have avoided.

"Bump on the head," he said, pointing to his temple.

"Well, come on," Moll said, leading him down the hallway, "Brian and Jan will be waiting."

Nathan pulled out of her grip. He didn't know who this Brian and Jan were, and anyway, he had more important things to do. He lifted the cup of hot chocolate for Moll to see. "Wait," he said. "I've got a hot chocolate here. I bumped into Mr. Hernandez. He asked me to get him one."

Moll frowned. "Looks like you bumped into more than Mr. Hernandez," she said. "Anyway, who's Mr. Hernandez?"

Nathan wandered back in the direction he'd come from. "My physics tutor," he said. "I told you about him."

Moll followed, grudgingly. "What physics tutor?" she said, genuinely baffled. "What was it you bumped your head on, Nathan? A truck?"

Nathan carried the paper cup back to where Mr. Hernandez still sat watching the TV.

"Thanks, Nathan," he said, no less cheerful than before.

"Who's that?" Moll asked.

"I told you. Mr. Hernandez."

"He looks like he's had a fight with a planet."

"Two, actually," answered Nathan.

Mr. Hernandez looked absentmindedly at Nathan, and at Moll. He noted Nathan's glum expression. He wrinkled his brow. "What's up, Nathan? Not the end of the world, is it?" he said, sipping the drink.

Nathan shook his head. He glanced at Moll, then in a low, conspiratorial voice he said, almost to himself: "That's just it, I don't know."

He crouched down beside Mr. Hernandez's chair.

"Listen, sir," he said, whispering so that Moll wouldn't hear. "Can I ask you something? Something about . . . time?"

The question came somewhat out of the blue, and the expression on Mr. Hernandez's face was almost precisely the expression of a physics teacher who, dosed to the eyeballs on painkillers, had just been asked if he was a banana.

Nathan felt almost sorry for him.

Moll shuffled closer. "Are you coming, Nathan?" she asked. "Brian and Jan, they'll be going soon. The doctors, they say Brian just had a sprained wrist." She made a move to go but stopped. Concern kept her there, close to Nathan. And affection.

"I mean," Nathan started again. "Time, is it fixed? What we know—we can't change it, can we? Or break it, or tear it apart or something? I mean, what if you go and change something that's already happened? Something that's not supposed to be changed?"

He was thinking of Henry and the Embankment and what Bartleby had told him.

It wasn't only Moll now who was staring at Nathan with a look of great concern. Mr. Hernandez was, too. He took a moment to sip his hot chocolate, then he adopted that overly friendly expression teachers save for overly sensitive pupils. His eyebrows almost disappeared from sight.

"Now Nathan," he said, leaning closer, "you've had a very hard time this last year. What with your mother and father, and the accident—" He stopped, licking the froth from his mustache. "It's understandable if you think everything's against you. That you can't rely on things to stay the same."

Nathan sighed. "I'm talking about the universe disappearing down the drain, sir," he said.

"Actually, what I think he's talking about is time travel," Moll said suddenly, with a jarring burst of clarity that momentarily stumped them all.

"What?" said Nathan.

"What?" asked Mr. Hernandez.

"I am?" Nathan said. Moll nodded sagely.

It was as though Moll had seen in one moment what Nathan had been scrambling around in the dark to find all along. She was right.

He was talking about time travel.

CHAPTER SIXTEEN

A BRIEF HISTORY OF TIME TRAVEL

Mr. Hernandez blinked.

"Are you what?" he said, his smile fading. "Sorry, Nathan, had an episode with two dogs earlier," he said, scratching at his neck brace. "Still a bit soggy in the old noggin, I'm afraid."

Moll stepped forward, swinging the bags of potato chips casually. "Time travel. You're talking about time travel," she said. "Going back in time to change something."

Nathan tried to arrange the conflicting thoughts that were rolling around his head like marbles. "What I'm trying to do . . ." He stopped. "What I'm trying to say,

Mr. Hernandez," he said, starting again, "is, if a man . . . if he goes back and does something in the past . . . goes to the past—"

"Travels in time," interrupted Moll. "To the past."

"Yes, travels back somehow," said Nathan. "If he goes and tries to change something, stops something terrible—something awful—from happening. Well, what happens? Now, I mean. To time? Will it be destroyed?"

Mr. Hernandez smiled. "Destroy time? No you can't destroy time. There isn't just one, you see. There are as many different times as there are stars in the sky, and all of them are different," he said. "The time we know is only one of them." He paused. "Nathan, have you heard of a man called Einstein?"

"The weird guy with the hair?"

"That's him. Well," said Mr. Hernandez, scratching his neck brace, "old Albert, he said that time wasn't fixed at all, see. He said it was changing all the, well, *time.* He saw space-time as a big mattress, and something enormous and heavy like the sun sits plumb in the middle of this space-time, like a bowling ball in the middle of a water bed."

"Then the sun and the planets and everything could be an orange, couldn't it?" Nathan said, thinking aloud. "And the mattress, it could be the peel."

Even as he said the words, he felt the nerves return to

his stomach. *Maybe it isn't so absurd,* he thought. The orange and its peel—maybe what Bartleby had said was true.

An idea blossomed in his mind then, an idea that had come to him while he was talking to the nurse, an idea so absurd he didn't want to believe it.

He got to his feet as the 2:30 race was won by a horse called Monkey Cake Baker.

Seeing this new resolve in his face, Moll snatched his wrist. "Look, Nathan," she said, "Brian and Jan, they'll be worried. I really—"

Nathan ignored her. "Mr. Hernandez," he said, "what if a man does go back in time? Could he change something?"

"There's no evidence that a man could go back—it's not like on TV—"

Nathan implored him. "But if he did!"

"Could he change something?" Mr. Hernandez muttered, as though he'd never really thought about it. "Well, I suppose so, yes. But we wouldn't be able to tell, would we?"

"We wouldn't?" Nathan said. "Why not?"

Mr. Hernandez's eyes appeared to cloud over again. "Well, we wouldn't," he said. "Because of what I said before about there being many different times. By acting, he would have made a new time, a new history. And it would be *our* new history too. Do you see?" He was struggling to describe a very complicated thing in a very simple way, and at the same time trying desperately to see straight. "From where we stand, Nathan, the future has all sorts of possibilities but the past only has one. The past is *fixed* in our history. Whatever your time traveler will have done in the past will be our history now. But we could never tell because in our history it will have already happened."

"Like if you went back in time and invented the combustion engine," said Moll, catching on, in her own way.

Mr. Hernandez nodded. Nathan still felt he was running to catch up.

"But if someone could tell?" he said. "If one person could tell the difference. Someone like me."

"Nathan," tried Moll, holding him tighter. She could see the tension pressing in on his eyes, making them look thin and pale, like almonds.

"Well, I don't know," said Mr. Hernandez, visibly perplexed. "The smallest incident in the past could alter the future in ways you can't predict," he said. He too had noticed the alarming intensity in Nathan's face. "B-but what is definite," he added, "is that things *would* be different. They might be big changes or small changes, but they'd be there if we looked. Every act has consequences, Nathan. Even if we don't mean them." He stopped and reflected on what he'd said. He smiled coyly to himself. "But really there's nothing to worry about, is there?" he said.

"There's not?" asked Nathan with surprise.

"Of course not, Nathan," said Mr. Hernandez. "I mean, if that were happening, and you could tell, Nathan, then you'd be able to see that things had changed, wouldn't you? You, Nathan Cobbe, would see that things were, a bit, well—"

"Counter clockwise," said Nathan.

"Exactly," Mr. Hernandez replied, smiling a toothless smile.

CHAPTER SEVENTEEN

THE SILENT CRIMES OF DAME AGATHA PORRITCH

Nathan turned to face Moll, who was still gripping his wrist.

"Then the world isn't being destroyed," he said, smiling. "Bartleby, he was wrong!"

"Bartleby?" said Moll.

"The Beefeater," Nathan gasped. He was consumed with a great sense of joy and relief. Mr. Hernandez was right. If Henry had changed time, then Nathan would have noticed. Things would be different. Sort of counter clockwise. And, as far as he could tell, things were the same. Certainly there were no dinosaurs roaming the halls of the hospital. The world hadn't been taken over by ants or monkeys. And the TV was still working.

"It wasn't real," he said, but it was with more emphasis than before, as though he were still trying to convince himself.

Mr. Hernandez's attention was lost among the froth of his hot chocolate. "A cookie would be nice with this, Nathan," he said, without any real hope.

Moll and Nathan stood facing each other, while on the TV The Elusive Pooh won the 2:30 from York by a short head. Moll didn't know what to think.

"Wasn't your grandpa a Beefeater?" she asked.

Nathan was hardly listening. He was too happy—in fact he was overjoyed. Everything was back to normal. Henry hadn't disappeared through a wall. He was here in the hospital. Bartleby was just a—just a hallucination, brought about by a bump on the head. Whatever he was, he wasn't real, Nathan told himself.

This was real: Moll and the hospital. Nurse Sheila. This was the real world:

Nathan's world!

Moll stared at him in bewilderment. She'd never seen him so excited, so overwhelmed. It frightened her. *Maybe it was the bump*, she thought. But even that couldn't explain the joyous look in his eyes, the laugh in his voice. She had to find someone who might help. Someone—anyone!

"Look, Brian and Jan," she said, tugging him by his hand, "they'll be going crazy with worry. Please, Nathan."

Nathan snapped his head around, the trace of that same smile remaining on his face.

"Who is this Brian and Jan you keep talking about, anyway?" he asked.

Moll almost broke down. "Brian and Jan Eckle," she said, her voice cracking. She cried, "Our *foster* mom and dad!"

Nathan said nothing.

It was a joke, he thought. But Moll wasn't the type to play jokes. He wanted to laugh, but the expression in her eyes stopped him.

"What do you mean?" he said.

"Haven't you seen him yet, Nathan?" Mr. Hernandez said. "Your dad?"

Nathan shook his head. Then something subsided in his stomach. Those old nerves again, they were waking up, stretching their wings like newborn moths, ready to take flight. All the certainty was gone in a flash.

"No, I couldn't find him," he said. "The nurse, she—"

Mr. Hernandez was only trying to be helpful when he nodded in the direction of the hallway and said, "He was just down there. Had his wrist bandaged. A sprain, was it?" he asked, peering up into Moll's ashen face.

She nodded without taking her eyes from Nathan.

"Nice guy," Mr. Hernandez continued, oblivious to the silent distress his words were causing. "Brian, he said his name was. Your foster dad, Nathan."

Nathan froze. He felt himself shaking, felt cold. And there was Moll's hand in his, tight as a spring.

"That's right," she said. Her voice was gentle, calm, trying to make him understand. "Brian and Jan Eckle," she said. "*Our* foster parents. Don't you remember, Nathan? I've been with them two years, you've been with them since the accident. Tonight we went out to watch the Christmas lights being turned on—that's how we got caught in the blackout. Remember? Oh, say you remember!" she said, her fingers tightening around his, urging him to understand.

"But . . ."

Moll trembled. She could feel the heat of his hand, and then there was the grayness in his face. She removed her hand from his and pressed it against his forehead.

"You're burning up," she said. "Look, if you're not coming, I'm going to get a nurse!"

Nathan couldn't hear her. The blood was pounding in his temples and there was a sickening noise in his head, a high-pitched moan, like the whine of the electric rails in the Underground. He felt faint. "But where's Henry?" he managed to say.

Mr. Hernandez's glazed eyes flickered behind his spectacles. "Henry?" he said, his voice sad and tender. "But Nathan, Henry's *dead*."

"Dead?"

This *was* no joke. Nathan could see that Mr. Hernandez was telling the truth. The awful and the terrible truth. Henry was dead.

"Yes, Nathan. He died in the accident. Don't you remember? Your mom and dad, they were hit by a bus on the Embankment, last year. They died. I'm sorry."

Nathan felt as though the world was collapsing upon him, pressing the air from his lungs. "He can't," he said. "They didn't . . ."

Mr. Hernandez's mustache trembled. "I really am sorry, Nathan."

Moll could wait no longer. If she was going to get help, she had to go now, she thought, before it was too late. "I'm going to get Brian and Jan," she said. "You wait here! Nathan, okay? Don't move!"

With that she flew headlong down the hall, darting between the stretchers and the throng of the walking wounded. Nathan didn't even notice her go. He saw nothing beyond the flickering of the ceiling lights and the pulsating of the TVs.

The man on TV said the 2:30 from Ripon was won by The Silent Crimes of Dame Agatha Porritch.

"Two-thirty," Nathan muttered, to no one in particular.

"What?" Mr. Hernandez hiccuped.

Nathan looked at his broken watch. "Two-thirty," he repeated, and something triggered then in the back of his mind. "It's two-thirty!"

Mr. Hernandez glanced at the clock on the TV. It said 6:05 P.M., but he said nothing. Somehow, he thought, he'd already said too much.

Nathan's shoulders shook, as though he were waking from sleep. He stared past the heads of the people waiting in the hallway, out to the exit. He wiped a hand across his eyes and found he was crying.

"I've got to go," he said. "Bartleby will be waiting for me!"

"Bartleby?"

Beyond the crowded hallway, beyond the automatic doors, Nathan could see the Christmas lights blinking. Something red slid by in the night.

Without a word of good-bye he broke into a run, rushing past Nurse Sheila, past the chipmunks, past the vending machine and the pale flickering TV screens, past the molelike man and his wife, past Moll and the Eckles, out to the emergency exit.

Mr. Hernandez sent him off with a cheerful wave. "Aren't you waiting for your dad, Nathan?" he yelled.

Nathan didn't stop.

"I don't think he'll be coming back anytime soon," he shouted before disappearing through the doors. Outside, it felt cold enough to snow. He ran toward the road, not knowing where he was headed—just running, from instinct.

He had been going for only a matter of seconds when a great light came up behind him. He heard brakes squeal across his shoulder. When he looked there was a bright, blinding light in his face. There was a *crash*. And a burst of thick, hot air filled his lungs. There was the smell of burning, and he could taste oil on his lips. Something was on fire.

He saw the driver's face and the number of the bus. Then there was a flash.

Then nothing at all for the longest time.

CHAPTER EIGHTEEN
A RETURN TICKET

Everywhere there was light.

Bright, white light, like snow, like sun. Electric light. It was so bright, it hurt Nathan's eyes to look at it. But he had no choice but to look, because Bartleby was speaking: He could hear his voice over the noise of the brakes, bringing him to consciousness.

Nathan had never seen anything so bright. It was so bright that he began to wonder if he was back in the Underground train at the moment of the flash of the explosion. But it wasn't only bright, it was alien, too—unearthly. It smelled alive and clean and beautiful, like the insides of a TV.

"... some men live in the past," Bartleby was saying. He sat facing the windows, and as Nathan watched him, the great Beefeater smiled at the stations passing by behind the glass. "And some men live in the future. Very few live in the present. But Henry has gone that one step further than other men, Nathan," he continued. "He is *returning* to the past. You see, time isn't a sequence, Nathan, it's an illusion. It is—"

Nathan interrupted him. "Nature's way of making sure everything doesn't happen at once," he said.

Bartleby nodded with pride and admiration. "Yes."

Nathan was back on the train. He could see the tunnel walls flash by, like years. And the stations, they were lit up: islands in the night.

"Are you all right?" asked Bartleby. "You look like you've seen a ghost."

"A ghost?" *Yes,* thought Nathan, *a ghost.*

But he wasn't frightened, not now. How could he be frightened when he was here with Bartleby? "Where did you go just now?" he asked.

Bartleby's eyes grew wide; they seemed to sparkle with warmth. "I went nowhere, Nathan," he said. "It was you. You blasted through the side of the train. Don't you remember?"

"Blasted?" repeated Nathan. "Like Henry?"

Bartleby nodded.

"Then what I just saw, at the hospital. That didn't happen?" Nathan asked. He was hoping Bartleby would tell him that it hadn't been real. That the hospital, like time, was an illusion. But Bartleby was not about to let him off so easily.

"It is all happening all the time," he answered.

"You mean it was the future?"

Bartleby's smile looked like it might never fade. He seemed serene, as might a man who had finally reached the point to which his life—or death—had been leading him. Nathan envied him. "Everything is *now*, Nathan," he said. "That was just an alternative now. The now where Henry died."

"But how?" asked Nathan. "How can we travel in time like that?"

"What do you think you're doing now? We're all time travelers, Nathan. Only most people choose to go in one direction," Bartleby said. "To the future. Very rarely does a man or woman come along and choose a different direction."

Nathan was catching on. "You mean Henry."

"Henry's no different from anyone else. He's just stuck in reverse," Bartleby said.

"Sort of counter clockwise," Nathan said, almost too quiet for Bartleby to hear.

"We are all time travelers," repeated Bartleby. "Only most of us don't know it."

The train roared on. Nathan looked at the other passengers in the car. He wondered if any of them realized that they too were time travelers, moving incrementally through the universe, all of them. He glanced up as another station flashed by.

"But you lied. The world—it isn't coming to an end, is it?" he said, suddenly remembering what Mr. Hernandez had said.

For an instant Bartleby's veneer cracked. He seemed genuinely uncertain. "Did I lie?" he asked. "Nathan, your life with Henry exists in one time, one history. It was created when Cornelle died. Each history is a new world, Nathan. A new *now*. And when it is destroyed, it is destroyed forever. Henry will destroy *this* world, Nathan. And I'm rather partial to it, that's all."

"But why?"

"I have my reasons," Bartleby said. "Two rather special reasons: you and Henry."

"I missed him," Nathan said. "I tried to stop him, but I was too late. He was gone before I could reach him. Then, at the hospital, he wasn't there. They said he was dead."

"Of course," said Bartleby. "Because he changed things. He went back, Nathan. To the Embankment. You were there. You heard it."

The *bang* in the traffic, the crowd standing around the bus.

"But what did he do?" Nathan asked.

"He tried to make things right."

At last Nathan understood, or at least he was beginning

to. "You mean Mom," he said. "He tried to save her life, didn't he? Stop her from being killed."

Bartleby didn't answer. He reached inside his tunic. Nathan watched as he brought out a large gold fob watch. "We're nearly there," Bartleby said.

"Where?" Nathan turned to the shadow pressing outside the glass. More stations flashed by. *Bartleby was right,* he thought. *It may as well be a journey through time, and each station a year.* But were they headed into the future or into the past? Then he remembered what Bartleby had said: how time was an orange peel, circle upon circle spinning farther downward. And he noticed something new, something he had not noticed before. "We're going the other way!" he said.

"We're going *backward,* Nathan, like Henry," Bartleby said. "Back to the Embankment." There was a strange yearning in the Beefeater's face. "Henry will be arriving soon," he added.

Nathan's heart began to beat faster, and he had a sickening sensation in his head. *Maybe this is what traveling through time feels like,* he thought. Maybe it just feels like trying very hard to remember something—like the details of your mom's face—until your brain feels like it might go *pop.*

"You have to stop him, Nathan," Bartleby said.

The train was going so fast now that Nathan couldn't bear to look out the windows. He closed his eyes and clapped his hands over his ears. But there was that whine in his head again, and a force, a terrible force pressing against his chest.

"*He's going to try to save your mother, but he doesn't understand, Nathan. Some things will not be changed,*" Bartleby continued. His voice seemed too deep, too resonant to be real. It began to take on the noise of the train until Nathan couldn't tell one from the other. Now Bartleby's voice was all around him and inside his head, like the roar of the engine and the screeching of the lines.

"*A very wise man once wrote,*" Bartleby's voice seemed to say—but it was no longer a voice; it was the air around him, the air in the tunnel and in the night. It was the air on the Embankment that was cold enough to snow. And it was the light, the blinding light—"*'The Moving Finger writes, and having writ, moves on: Nor all your Piety nor Wit shall lure it back to cancel half a Line, nor all your Tears wash out a Word of it. . . .*'"

Nathan braced himself. He waited for the flash and the smell of oil and burning. He didn't think he would ever get used to it, the shock of the journey. But even as he thought it, the sickness seemed to subside. And the flash was no longer so shocking.

There was only the smell of snow. It was clean and fresh and invigorating. And there were the lights, sparkling like stars.

He opened his eyes.

CHAPTER NINETEEN

MOM

It was afternoon on the Embankment.

The road was busy with traffic, and the car headlights shone against the falling snow. It whirled and spun in the air like moths in moonlight. The sky was overcast and gray, but as the clouds rolled back, they broke at times with sunlight, and there were glimpses of blue at the edges of the storm. The snow would pass.

Nathan shivered from the cold. He wasn't dressed for the weather. Rain was dripping from the Underground station roof and falling down his neck, and he shuddered and took a step into the road, careful of the umbrellas of the passersby.

The sidewalks were bustling with people running blind, trying to escape the snowfall, and Nathan had to fight to stay upright. He barely had a chance to admire the Christmas lights that were strung out across the road, hanging from the streetlights and fizzing and flashing against the bruised gray clouds.

He hesitated, resisting the pull of the crowd. He didn't want to get ahead of himself. He had to be patient.

The traffic had pulled to a halt, and Nathan thought he heard something up ahead. A car horn sounded.

Please don't let me be late, Nathan prayed, craning his neck to see what was holding up the traffic. He was just about to set off down the sidewalk when a man in a wet gray suit bumped into him. He was knocked sideways and lost his footing on the sidewalk. For a moment the glare of the headlights from the traffic blinded him. Nathan imagined he saw the man turn briefly to apologize. Then all he saw was the back of the man's squareish balding head as he ran on, disappearing into the crowds.

"Dad!"

It was Henry, the same Henry who had disappeared through the bathroom wall only moments ago.

"Dad!" Nathan yelled, struggling to his feet. He pushed past the crowd.

"Watch out," said one of the passersby.

"Careful," warned another.

"Mind yourself, kid!"

But Nathan was deaf to them. In the distance he could see Henry's balding head bobbing in the crowd. He was going fast, too fast for Nathan to catch up. No matter how hard he tried, he was losing ground; he was all but losing hope, too, when Henry stopped dead on the sidewalk.

Henry had turned to face the road, as though he were expecting something to arrive. *His face looks awful,* Nathan thought. It was ashen, and there was a horror in his eyes that made Nathan shake. As he stood there, a red shadow seemed to pass over his face. And Nathan saw what Henry saw:

It was a bus.

A red Routemaster bus, heading down the Embankment!

Mom, Nathan thought, and he found he was running down the gutter, past the crowds on the sidewalk, past the cars moving past only inches from him.

Henry was running now too. Seeing the bus, he had stepped down from the sidewalk and pushed on into the road, causing the oncoming traffic to screech to a halt. Horns blared out. Brakes screamed. Drivers leaned out of their windows and yelled at him.

Henry didn't stop. But the bus was already past him; it was past them both, rolling on down the road.

Down toward . . .

Mom!

Nathan could see her now. She was standing on the curb, searching in her bag for something. Her hair was wet with the rain, and she was wearing the green coat with the fake fur collar that she liked so much, the one Henry had bought her for her birthday. She couldn't have been more than forty yards away down the Embankment.

She was here—his mom, Cornelle.

And she was alive!

It had been so long since Nathan had seen her, he'd almost forgotten what she looked like. Over the months, he'd tried to hold on to the memory of her eyes, her nose, but over time they had faded, until all he could remember was the smile—the smile she used for photographs. Like the one on the mantelpiece. A false memory. Not Mom at all. But it was all he'd had.

Until now.

"Mom?" he called out. He had staggered to a stop. He was too far away now, and too slow; he knew he would never catch up.

"Mom!" He almost lost sight of her as the bus moved into view. But he could see Henry. He was maybe twenty feet away from her now. If only Cornelle had looked up, she would have seen him barreling down the sidewalk toward her. But she was too busy trying to pull her umbrella out of her bag. It was raining harder now, as the bus approached. And the sunlight was bouncing up from the puddles in the road and what was left of the snow.

Suddenly Henry stopped. He too had seen Cornelle standing by the road. It had thrown him. The sight of her here, alive! As though he'd woken from a dream.

"Henry!" gasped Nathan, stumbling forward.

The bus was still gaining speed. And Cornelle, she'd removed the umbrella now and was fumbling with it, trying to get it to open. She wasn't paying attention to the traffic, to the bus rumbling toward her. She hadn't seen.

But Nathan had. He saw it all.

Time seemed to stop for him. He saw the bus, and Henry, and his mother. And all the while the words of Bartleby were echoing in his mind.

The Moving Finger writes, and having writ, moves on . . .

He knew what he had to do; what he was here to do. He knew he had stop Henry. But seeing his mother, seeing her so alive, so real—he couldn't do it. He wanted her to live, wanted her back. Nothing in the world at that moment would have changed his mind.

And Henry could do it. He could save her, Nathan knew it. He was only feet away. Yet he was frozen to the spot.

Nathan could see it all: the bus and Henry and Mom!

"Henry!" he screamed. "Henry! The bus!"

In the distance, in the rain, Henry half turned, hearing his name. He looked around, not knowing who might have called out, breaking him from his reverie.

And he saw the bus, and he remembered! *Cornelle! He had to save her!*

Henry lurched forward, pushing past the figures on the sidewalk, past the rain and the spraying water. He was alongside the bus now. Cornelle was already stepping down into the road. Her umbrella had blown inside out, shielding her from the glare of the bus's headlights.

The bus had no time to stop. It was wet, and with the sunlight in the road, the driver didn't stand a chance. It was only when Henry ran into the road that he braked. The bus's wheels skidded in the puddles.

Nathan saw Henry grab Cornelle in his arms. For a moment he thought it was possible. Nathan thought there was a chance they might escape the bus. But he was wrong. He saw them exchange a frozen, startled look before the bus careened—

He saw them embrace.

Then there was a great flash of light. A *bang* that made his blood run cold: the sound of a collision, the crash before a long, dead silence. Someone screamed. Then the lights . . .

. . . Nor all your Piety nor Wit shall lure it back to cancel half a Line, nor all your Tears wash out a Word of it. . . .

Then nothing for the longest time.

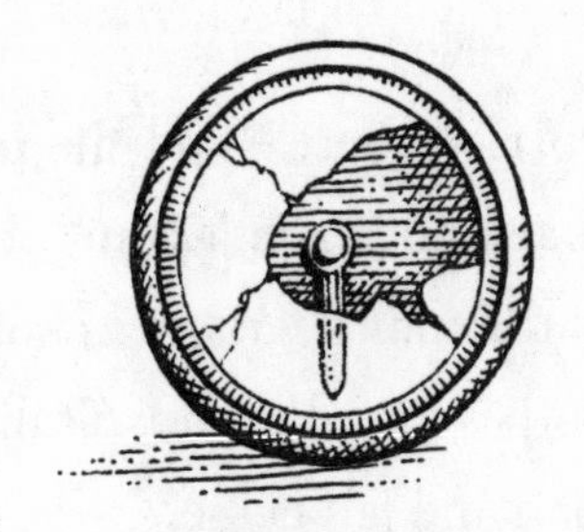

CHAPTER TWENTY

HOME

"Is he awake?"

Light. And the smell, like the insides of a TV.

He opened his eyes.

For a moment he could see only the white of the walls, and the ceiling. Then a pleasant-looking man and woman in matching sweaters were standing over him. They were smiling. But their smiles could not hide the concern in their faces.

"Is he awake?" asked a voice behind them—a girl's voice.

"He is now," said the man and woman together. Then the girl joined them.

It was Moll.

"Hello, Nathan," said Moll. The pleasant-looking woman put an arm around her and squeezed her tight. They stood there, the three of them. Close, as only a family can be.

"You had us worried there," said the pleasant-looking man. "But you're back now, aren't you?"

Nathan noticed the man's wrist was bandaged. He recognized them both from the hospital, the man and woman. It was Brian and Jan Eckle.

Nathan nodded.

"Yeah," he said. "I'm back."

CHAPTER TWENTY-ONE

THE DOG WHO BLEW BUBBLES

It was two weeks before Nathan was allowed home. When the day arrived, Brian and Jan helped him gingerly into their little car. It was a weekday, so Brian drove them out to the school, where Moll was waiting by the gates. Then all four drove back to Acacia Avenue.

The Eckles had a large ramshackle house at the end of the street. It was set back from the road by an overgrown garden littered with fallen rotten fruit and mushrooms, brambles and old tennis balls. There was a lean-to garage to one side of the house. Behind the house, through the broken hedgerows and over the ditch, there was a long, narrow strip of communal land they called the common, where the Eckles would take their new pet gray-faced pug, Fidget, whom they'd just gotten from the dog rescue shelter, letting him run riot among the wild grasses and bushes.

Nathan had never had a dog before, and Moll had to show him how to pat Fidget so Nathan wouldn't scare or unsettle him—although Nathan couldn't imagine anything that would scare the ferocious little Fidget. From what he'd seen of him, he was a true little devil.

"He's had a hard life," Moll explained, every time Fidget snarled or spat. "Honestly, he's calmed down since we got him."

Not that Fidget frightened Nathan, despite his temper. After all, Nathan had known the mighty Marbles, and nothing could be more vicious than Marbles. Instinctively, he pulled a stick of Bubble-Lite gum from his pocket and tossed it to Fidget, who caught it with a snap of his jaws with the same delinquent glee as that other gray-faced pug. In a moment he was chewing happily.

"I've never known a dog to like chewing gum before," Moll said, surprised by how benign Fidget had suddenly become.

"Oh, I've known one," Nathan said, patting the little terror on his scarred nose as the dog began to blow an impressive pineapple-flavored bubble. "A crazy thing called Marbles," he added, and he could have sworn the gray-faced pug blinked at the mention of the name. "Where'd you get him?" he asked, curious.

"Rescue shelter picked him up in Peckham," Moll answered.

Nathan smiled at the dog's familiar black eyes. "Figures," he said.

There was something familiar about Nathan's room, too. It was much the same as every room he'd ever slept in, dark and a little sweaty. Brian and Jan said they'd been meaning to "fix it up" ever since Nathan had come to live with them a year ago, and they promised they'd finally get around to it soon. "In fact I'm going to buy the paint today," Brian said, before he and Jan went downstairs, leaving Nathan by himself for a while. They were trying hard, he could tell.

It was when he was alone that Nathan found the photograph. It was in a cardboard box under the bed. On the side of the box someone had written, in marker, OLD STUFF.

Inside were all the things from his other life, before the accident. They were dusty and looked old somehow, forgotten. There was a mug that must have belonged to Henry, and Cornelle's bright red gloves. There was an old TV remote control and a pair of yellow socks. And there was a photo. It was an old, creased black-and-white photograph of a very large and very heavy-looking Beefeater:

Bartleby!

He appeared a little younger, and a little slimmer, but it was definitely Bartleby. He was holding his ceremonial pike in one hand, and in his free arm he was cradling a small baby.

Nathan turned over the photograph. On the back was a name written in Cornelle's handwriting:

Grandpa Cobbe

Grandpa?

Nathan read the note a second time. He looked at the face in the photograph. Bartleby's face. Bartleby was Nathan's *grandfather*. Henry's father—Bartleby Cobb.

Nathan should have been shocked, but then, had he really not suspected? In fact on the train, before the explosion, hadn't Bartleby tried to tell him as much? Hadn't Nathan realized then? With all the different times jumbling up against one another, it was hard to remember.

It must have been Henry's photo, Nathan realized. Something that had been hidden like a lie for years, lost in the back of a drawer or inside a book. He wondered who the baby was. It was hard to tell from the photo—the baby's face was faded and out of focus. Maybe it was Henry.

Nathan stared at the photo for most of the afternoon, going over in his mind the events of the last few days, or was it years? He could no longer tell. Then he packed all the things in the box again and carried it to the closet, where the box wouldn't get so dusty.

He opened the closet and placed the box in the back, under the piles of socks and shirts. It was narrow and dark, and Nathan found it difficult to maneuver the box, especially as he had the use of only one good arm. His right arm had been fractured in the incident outside the hospital, and it was in a plaster cast.

Nathan was itching for the cast to be taken off, and by the time, one Sunday in mid-December, he and Moll walked around the side of the house toward the common, he could already use his arm for holding a spoon and he could even throw Fidget his newest tennis ball. The bruises and scratches had healed too. All there was to show that Nathan had ever been in an accident was the cast.

"Don't go too far!" called Jan, leaning out from the attic window, seeing them go. "Dinner will be ready soon."

"We won't," Moll called back.

Out in the garage Brian was busy painting an old chest of drawers that they were planning to put in Nathan's room. Fidget was there too. Seeing Moll and Nathan, Fidget scampered out from the garage. Moll tossed him the tennis ball, and he caught it in his mouth and padded happily alongside them. *He really has mellowed,* thought Nathan.

"What do you think of the color?" Brian asked as they passed by. He held up the can of paint. It was called apple-blossom green, but Nathan thought it was more like radioactive green.

Nathan nodded. "Very . . . *green,*" he said.

Brian grinned proudly, as though "very green" were the greatest compliment one man could offer another. He went back to work, dipping his brush in the can of paint and slapping it happily against the chest of drawers.

"Come on, Marb—I mean, Fidget!" Nathan called, catching himself. They climbed through the hedge and down across the ditch to the common. Fidget dashed ahead, disappearing into the undergrowth.

It was almost Christmas, but on the common Nathan thought it seemed more like autumn. A soft blanket of mist had settled over the horizon, and all they could see of the city were a few office-block roofs poking up from the pale gloom. It was as if they were above the city, somewhere among the clouds where the air was fresh and smelled of blackberries and crab apples. Nathan loved it. The week he'd spent with the Eckles had been the nicest he could remember. Their house was a little oasis of calm in the city. He didn't know how they did it, but Brian and Jan made everything seem leisurely and peaceful, as though they brought their own quiet with them wherever they went.

He loved having Fidget to play with as well. And then, of course, there was Moll.

Since the accident Nathan and Moll had become close friends. It was as though Nathan had known her forever. Which, he reasoned, he had, in a way, in this *now*. A year at least. They talked together about everything under the sun. Things they liked and things they hated. There was very little they hadn't talked about—except for the night of the blackout. Nathan had hardly touched upon it. He still didn't know how to explain it all to her. In truth it all seemed like a dream now. His life with Henry was like a dream, as if it had never happened.

Which, of course, it hadn't, he told himself. In *this* now.

In this now Henry had died with Mom, trying to save her.

Nathan had to keep reminding himself of this every time he opened his mouth. He didn't want Moll to think he was crazy. It had been bad enough that night in the hospital; luckily, Moll had already attributed that to the bump on the head.

"What do you remember?" she asked, as they watched Fidget dash in and out of the bushes, searching for the tennis ball.

"I can't remember a thing," Nathan replied.

"The driver didn't see you till the last minute," Moll said very gently. Gentle wasn't something Moll was good at, but she'd heard on TV how you had to be very careful what you say around people who'd been through trauma because they might go loopy.

"You just ran straight out of the hospital," she said, "straight into the road. You're lucky he managed to brake at all."

Nathan picked up an old apple and tossed it into the heart of the mist. It disappeared. He waited for the sound of it falling amongst the bushes, but there was no sound. The mist had swallowed it up.

"You were acting really weird," Moll added, eyeing him. "Talking about Henry."

Nathan stopped. "Henry?"

He hadn't heard that name spoken in what seemed like a very long time.

"You seemed different."

"What do you mean, different?"

Moll shrugged. She picked up a stone and threw it into the mist. There was a soft thud as it landed in the dirt. "I don't know," she said. "It was like you didn't know me. Like we weren't, you know, friends."

She gave him a nervous look, and she took his hand.

Her hand was warm in his. And his mind went back once more to the hospital. "Sorry," he said.

Fidget came bounding back to them, holding the apple Nathan had thrown in his wet mouth. Nathan laughed seeing him. He broke away from Moll and took the apple and threw it again for Fidget, as far as he could.

"Do you think," he started, "do you think it's possible to forget things that happened in the past?"

"What things?" asked Moll. She laughed to herself as she watched Fidget bounce in and out of the mist.

Nathan was thinking of the accident on the Embankment. He was thinking of his life with Henry, in the apartment. Of the worried expression on Henry's face each morning.

"Bad things that have happened," Nathan answered. "Like what happened with your dad."

Moll turned to him. "I wouldn't want to," she said matter-of-factly. The ground was covered with rotten apples that had fallen from a nearby tree, and she bent down to pick them up. Then she tossed them one at a time into the mist for Fidget to chase.

Nathan joined her. "Why not?" he asked.

"Because I want to remember everything I can. It's all I've got left of him."

"Even if it hurts?"

Moll didn't answer that. She didn't have to. Nathan knew the answer; he could see it in her face. There was nothing that could have made her forget. Even the hurt. He was her *father*, after all.

"Moll! Nathan!" Jan's voice came singing over from the house.

"Come on!" Moll laughed, breaking into a run. "Last one is a rotten egg!"

They were both laughing so hard by the time they reached the ditch that they were out of breath, and they could only stumble through the hedgerows. Fidget was already across the yard and rocketing through the kitchen door, his coat wet and covered in weeds and mud.

Nathan paused to catch his breath before heading inside. "Who's that?" he asked, seeing a wiry figure toiling away in the garden next door. It was an old man. He was raking leaves. He was crooked and unkempt, and—Nathan thought—somehow familiar.

Moll turned to look.

"That's old Godfrey," she said, sitting down on the kitchen step, and pulling off her muddy boots. "He lives at Number Twenty-nine. His wife died ten years ago and he's never gotten over it. That's what Jan says. He works over at the New Cross—"

"—Hill Community College," finished Nathan.

"Yeah, that's right," said Moll. She dropped her boots by the doormat and then went into the house.

The old man let out a hacking cough. He dropped his rake. Nathan took a moment to see that he had managed to pick it up again, and then followed Moll indoors.

CHAPTER TWENTY-TWO

A WELCOME LETTER

"Eat up, Nathan!"

Jan dished up the roast potatoes while Brian sliced the turkey. There were mashed potatoes, too. And red cabbage. And roasted parsnips. And honeyed carrots. There was cranberry sauce and five different kinds of relish. There was chestnut stuffing, and sage-and-onion stuffing, and there was a large gravy boat brimming with hot turkey gravy. Everything smelled wonderful. It looked wonderful. It tasted even better.

Sitting there, in Brian and Jan's kitchen, Nathan felt he had entered some secret lottery—the family lottery. And he had won. He felt safe—safe in ways he could never have imagined feeling in Tarside. It was quiet and warm, and each morning when he woke, he could hear birds on the common. The sound of the traffic was there, of course—it was everywhere in London—but somehow, the birdsong here muffled it.

Nathan realized that he was *happy*.

Yet something was holding him back from enjoying himself completely. It wasn't that he felt he didn't deserve it. Everyone deserved this sort of family, this sort of life, he reasoned. Otherwise, what was life for? And it wasn't that he felt guilty, either. It was just that . . . it didn't seem right: his being here, with the Eckles. No matter how nice they were. No matter how much he liked them, and Moll. He hardly dared admit it to himself, because he was so happy. But the truth was, he didn't *belong* here.

He belonged in the other "now." The now where he had succeeded in stopping Henry on the Embankment. He belonged at Tarside, with Henry.

But Nathan didn't even know if that "now" existed anymore. What if it didn't? What then? And worse than that, Nathan knew that there was a small part of him that *wanted* it to no longer exist. Then, at least, he could stay here with the Eckles, with Moll. He could stay happy.

And that made him feel worse.

"Get down, Fidget!" Brian laughed, throwing Fidget a piece of turkey. "There, that should keep you quiet.

Nathan, we'll get your room fixed up this week," he added as the front doorbell rang. "Oh, who could that be?"

"I'll get it," said Jan, standing up from the table. Nathan watched her go down the hall to the door. From where he was sitting, he could see into the porch. When she opened the door, he recognized Godfrey Pooter standing there. In his hand he was holding something, which he gave to Jan. Then he smiled and tipped his cap.

"Thank you, Godfrey," Jan said, waving him off. She shut the door.

"That was Godfrey," she said, returning to the table. "He says yesterday the mailman gave him a letter meant for us by mistake. He only just remembered. It's addressed to you, Moll," she added, and she handed Moll a very formal-looking white envelope.

Moll peered at it. She seemed taken aback.

It was a normal envelope, the kind you buy in any shop. Yet it was different in some way. Everyone felt it. And Nathan and Brian and Jan and Fidget were all looking Moll's way, waiting for her to open it.

Moll felt suddenly important, and a little scared. It was as if they had all sensed that something extraordinary was about to happen, only they didn't know what. They held their breath as Moll tore at the edge of the envelope. She pulled out a piece of square letter paper. It was folded in half, and Moll unfolded it and began to read it quietly to herself.

Everyone waited.

When Moll was finished, she reread the letter; then she looked up at Brian and Jan and Nathan. And she screamed! Nathan jumped in his chair. But in a moment he was on his feet, jumping up and down. Moll was jumping too. Everyone was jumping. Even Fidget. Moll was laughing and screaming and waving the letter as if it were a check for a million pounds.

"It's Dad!" she yelled, her eyes filling with tears. "They've found him. I knew he didn't die, I knew it!" She ran up to hug Brian. Then she went to Jan and kissed her on her cheek. Jan took the letter and began to read it herself.

"It says he was in an accident. He lost his memory. But he's okay now. He's flying home next week!" she said, glancing up at Brian and then at Nathan. She was crying.

It was the most amazing news Nathan could imagine.

Moll had her father back! Or would have, in a week's time. She was ecstatic. More than that, she'd been proved right: All along she'd refused to believe her father had died. She knew he was alive, and now her faith had been vindicated.

She'd been right, Nathan thought, later that night. *She'd been right not to forget.*

He was sitting alone at the top of the stairs, thinking about everything that had happened. After the revelation of the letter, the dinner had turned into a party for Moll. Brian and Jan had put on some music, and Nathan had watched Moll and Brian and Jan dance around in the kitchen. They'd forgotten all about the turkey. No one noticed Fidget climb onto the table and nibble at the uneaten food.

They'd danced on into the night. At midnight, Brian had taken the trifle out from the fridge, and they had all sat down for a midnight feast. Then they'd gone to bed.

But Nathan hadn't been able to sleep. His mind was churning with thoughts and ideas. Memories. He remembered the journey in the Underground, to the Embankment. And he remembered what Bartleby had said about the Moving Finger.

The Moving Finger was time. That's what Bartleby had tried to tell him. And time could not be shaped by Nathan, or Henry.

Nor all your Piety nor Wit shall lure it back to cancel half a Line. . . .

Henry had tried to cancel it and failed. And now he was gone.

The floorboards on the landing creaked. Nathan turned. "Hello?" he whispered. The door to Moll's room opened and she stepped out.

"Nathan?" she whispered. She was dressed in her pajamas.

"You can't sleep either?" he said.

Moll shook her head. She joined Nathan, squeezing next

to him on the top step. He noticed she was wearing the same grateful expression she had been wearing since she'd opened the envelope. Nathan doubted it would ever leave her.

"He'll be here next week," she said, lost in the wonder and the shock of it all. "I can go live with him. We'll have Christmas together!"

Nathan couldn't help but be happy for her. But he was sad, too. And despite his smile, Moll noticed it.

"I'll come back and see you," she said, trying to reassure him. "And we'll see each other at school." But she knew it didn't sound like much comfort. Nathan would still be alone with the Eckles.

"It's not that," Nathan said, with feeling. Moll believed him.

"I'm just thinking about Mom and Dad," he said. "It's just, I can't remember what Mom looked like. I mean, I can see her, but I can't remember exactly what her nose was like, or her eyes. I can just remember her smile."

Moll nodded. "I know," she said. "It's the same with Dad. It's been two years."

"But you'll be seeing him next week."

Moll beamed.

Nathan felt a little better, seeing Moll so happy. "What did Brian and Jan tell you about what happened to my mom and dad?" he asked. "How they died."

"Well, it was a road accident, wasn't it? And they . . . well, you know."

Nathan turned on the stair and looked directly into Moll's face. "But what if they didn't?" he said. "What if they didn't die? What if there was a mistake, like with your dad? What if Henry's still alive somewhere?"

Moll didn't know what to say right away. Nathan was looking at her so intently.

"Moll," he said, "I don't think I'm meant to be here."

Moll glanced down the stairs at the splash of moonlight on the hall carpet. "But Jan and Brian, they're so nice," she said. "It's great here. And I promise, Nathan, I'll come back and see you. You won't be alone."

Nathan shook his head. He grabbed her hand. "No," he said, "I don't mean that. I don't think I'm meant to be here, *now*. Henry—he's still alive. I know he is, Moll. He's alive somewhere. You see, there *was* a mistake. I made a mistake, and Henry disappeared, and everything I knew changed. And now I've got to get back to him."

He saw the struggle in Moll's face. It was the same expression he'd seen in the hospital. "It's like you said about your dad," he went on. "If you could go back and stop him from stepping out of the door that day, the day he disappeared, you would have, wouldn't you? You'd have done anything to stop him. Even now."

"Yes," Moll said. Her expression was changing, softening. She squeezed his hand.

"You don't think I'm crazy, do you?" he asked.

"No."

"Then that's what I have to do. I have to stop him," Nathan said. "Don't I?"

Moll looked down at his fingers, which were nestled in hers. She let go of his hand. "If you think Henry's still alive, then you have to go find him, Nathan," she said. "You have to."

One week later a large white car parked outside the Eckles' house. From his window Nathan watched Moll run out from the garden and into the avenue. He watched as the car door opened and a tall, slim man climbed out. He watched as the man and Moll hesitated, seeing each other. Then the man reached out his arms and Moll ran into them.

"Dad!" she said.

They got into the car. Nathan stepped back from the window as the car engine started up. He sat on his bed and listened to the sounds of the house without Moll in it. Downstairs a door slammed.

Then he heard footsteps on the stairs. Suddenly Moll was in the doorway. He stood up and hugged her. Then she was gone again.

By the time he heard the car driving away, Nathan had made up his mind.

He was going to stop Henry, once and for all.

CHAPTER TWENTY-THREE

THE COBBS OF TARSIDE HEIGHTS

The next day was a Monday. Nathan's cast wouldn't be removed until the end of the week, but it was decided that he could go back for the last day of school on Wednesday. He had hardly been out of the house since he'd arrived from the hospital, so Nathan figured Brian and Jan might not raise too many objections if he asked to go somewhere. They wouldn't think it was suspicious.

Nathan and Brian were making the finishing touches to Nathan's room. They had finished hanging the curtains and arranging the furniture, and were standing back to admire the peculiar effect of the radioactive green furniture and the cream-colored walls, when Nathan said, "Brian?"

"Yes?" said Brian.

"I'm okay now, aren't I?" Nathan said. "Except for the cast. And I can get by okay with that."

Brian agreed. "Yes, Nathan," he said. "You're perfectly fine." He straightened the curtains and made one last adjustment to the positioning of the desk in the corner. Christmas was only a week away, and Brian had even gone to the trouble of going out and buying Nathan a tiny Christmas tree for the room. They'd decorated it with bits of tinsel and an ornament; one tiny silver ball was all that the puny little thing could hold. But it was a nice thought.

"So what do you think of the room?" asked Brian.

"It's great," said Nathan.

"Really?" asked Brian hopefully.

Nathan nodded. It *was* great.

"Good." Brian sighed, satisfied he had done his best. "Sorry, Nathan, you were going to ask something?"

Nathan hesitated. "I thought, now that I'm okay again. I thought . . ."

"Yes, Nathan?"

"I wondered if I could go into the city. Before I start school."

"Of course," said Brian. "We could go look at the sights. Even visit the Tower of London," he added with enthusiasm. "Apparently the ravens have flown off—there's all kinds of stories on the TV, I can tell you—"

"The ravens?"

"That's right," Brian replied. "They've upped and gone. Yeah, I'll ask Jan if she'd like to go too. We could make a day of it, all three of us, okay?"

Nathan frowned, thinking about the ravens and what it meant. "Actually, I thought I might go into the city *by myself*," he said.

"Oh." Brian paused, weighing the idea.

"Maybe I could go in with Godfrey tomorrow when he goes to work?" Nathan said.

"Well, you'll have to check with Jan first, of course," said Brian. "But I don't see why not."

"Really?" cried Nathan.

Brian put his hand on Nathan's shoulder. He was surprised by how anxious Nathan seemed at the prospect of a day out, but he hid his concern. "Of course," he said. "Just make sure you watch out for the traffic, will you? And Nathan, try to come back in one piece!"

The next afternoon Nathan went to Godfrey's house. He found him puttering around with his little Volkswagen in the drive, checking the oil and cleaning the windshield wipers. He looked happy to have a companion with whom to share the journey to work. He even winked as he opened the passenger door.

"Shall we go then?" he said.

"Godfrey?" asked Nathan, once they were heading toward Peckham.

"Yes, Nathan?"

"You know the college, Godfrey?" he said.

"Yes?"

"Have you ever seen a Beefeater there?"

Godfrey cleared his throat and gave Nathan a long sideways glance.

Nathan shrugged. "Never mind," he said. "Oh, here," he said, seeing they were almost at Peckham High Street. "You can drop me off here, if you like!"

Godfrey pulled the Volkswagen into the curb.

"You sure you don't still feel a bit woozy?" Godfrey asked, as Nathan climbed out.

"No, I'm fine," Nathan replied.

Godfrey wasn't at all reassured, but he let it go. "I'll meet you at the college at six, all right?" he said.

Nathan nodded. He shut the car door. "Say hello to Enid for me!" he called as Godfrey pulled away. Nathan saw the old man blink in surprise, then shake his head irritably. The little car kangarooed down the road and across the intersection. After Nathan watched it go, he turned down the street, walking toward the project at Tarside.

That's when he noticed it: The apartments—they weren't there.

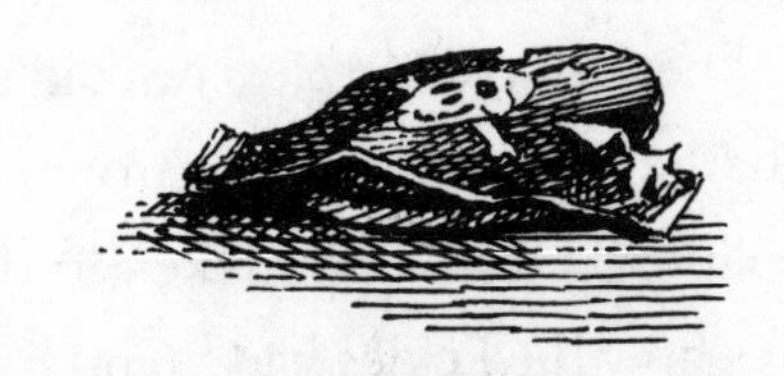

CHAPTER TWENTY-FOUR
COUNTER-CLOCK WORLD

Nathan hadn't known quite what to expect. He knew he couldn't expect everything to be the same. After all, this wasn't *his* now. It was the other now—the now in which Henry died. Small things would have changed; he knew that. It was like Mr. Hernandez had said: The smallest incident in the past could alter the future in ways you can't predict.

But he hadn't expected this. . . .

The project, it was *gone*. Completely gone. The towers, the parking lot, the stairs, and the narrow little underground walkway that cut through the grass bank and always smelled of pee, where no one ever walked.

Gone.

Then he remembered the date. It was mid-December. The scheduled demolition had been completed. That's why the three towers of Tarside were nowhere to be seen. It was why the crane was gone, and why the place where the parking lot and the courtyard had once been was now filled with rubble. Even Charlie and Turps were gone. And Marbles, too. But then, he knew where Marbles was, didn't he?

Turps and Charlie must have been thrown off the site before the demolition, and Marbles taken to the dog rescue shelter. That's how the Eckles had found him.

It all made sense, yet . . . *It's all so different,* he thought. Again he had to remind himself that it wasn't *his* now. He had never even lived here in *this* now. Henry had lived here, alone. All the stuff that had been collected in the box in the closet must have come from Cornelle's house and Henry's apartment. Given to Nathan as mementos after they'd died.

Then the Nathan of this now had gone to live with the Eckles. That's all the Nathan of this now knew. But still, as he walked among the rubble, the broken bricks and plaster, the cracked sinks, the mangled steel and ruined concrete, Nathan couldn't help but be disturbed.

Because he had *lived* here, in the other now. In Apartment 134 Tarside Heights, Peckham. He'd lived here with Henry.

And now it was all broken.

He kicked at a brick on the ground, heard its little *clunk* as it rolled down the slope of rubble. He watched it roll all the way down to the Dumpster.

The Dumpster.

It was standing there, sticking out from the debris like a sunken ocean liner. The record-breaking Dumpster. The Tarside Dumpster.

Nathan staggered down, sliding and tripping down the mound of rubble, until his hands slapped against its steel side. It was exactly the same as before except for the fact that it wasn't on fire. But it was the same. Of that he was sure.

To Nathan it was a large, rather smelly but touching souvenir of another life—a different life. A different time. He held on to it for a few moments, as though hugging a long-lost friend. A long-lost, rather smelly friend.

The fire had burned out long ago, and people had begun to dump their garbage in it again. There was an old punctured football and a chair with three legs, and he was surprised to see, half hidden under a broken TV set, a tattered paper pirate's hat. Charlie's hat. Nathan pulled it out and planted it on his head in tribute to his old friends. Then he rummaged some more, wondering what other gems he might find. But he wasn't in the least prepared for what he *did* find.

Most of the contents of the Dumpster was worthless junk that had been tossed out by the folks living nearby, but there was one item that caught Nathan's eye. It was a bundle of mail. All the envelopes were addressed to the apartments of Tarside Heights. Nathan guessed that since the apartments had been demolished, the mailman must have dumped them knowing that there was little chance they would ever now find their owners. Maybe the mailman thought there was a chance the owners would come around for one last look at the demolition site and find their mail. Maybe he didn't care.

There were seven envelopes that were addressed to Henry Cobbe of Apartment 134 Tarside Heights, Peckham.

Nathan checked the envelopes. Six of them were from the city government, but the third was handwritten. Nathan recognized the writing immediately as his mom's—Cornelle's. All of them were stamped LOST IN TRANSIT.

According to the postmark date on his mom's envelope, she had mailed it the day she died. He felt a long, low surge of emotion well up inside him, and he had to grit his teeth so he wouldn't cry. He pondered whether he should open it or not, whether the letter was his to read. It was Henry's, after all, sent to him from his ex-wife, the day she was run over.

But Henry was dead too, Nathan reminded himself.

His fingers were trembling as he pulled open the square blue envelope and slid out the neatly written letter. It read:

Dear Henry,

It was wonderful seeing you this morning, my love. And, in answer to your question, yes, I do feel we can get back together again, like you want. But give me a few days to break it to Nathan.

I know you are trying hard to prove yourself to him and to me, but don't work too hard. Please take care of yourself.

Remember: Your first duty is to stay safe and healthy so you can be a father to Nathan.

Love always,
Cornelle x

Nathan held the letter in his hands for a long, long time. He was still holding it when the workmen came back from their lunch break and started up the engines of their bulldozers, to clear the site.

A large, heavyset man dressed in a fluorescent jacket and helmet who was clearly the site manager ushered him politely out of the area and back to the main road.

Nathan stood at the side of the road, listening to the traffic. He was stunned.

Henry and Cornelle—they had agreed to get back together. Even live together again, possibly. As a family.

They had been secretly meeting behind his back, talking and planning. And Nathan had never known.

He felt exhausted. He felt as if he had run ahead of the whole world, and all he wanted to do now was sit down and wait for it to catch up with him. Wait for it to resume. *There's been a technical malfunction, like on TV*, he thought, *and any minute now, normal service will resume*. If only he waited. If only he was patient.

But he knew that was nonsense. He knew nothing would change. Not now.

Unless *he* changed it.

Unless, he thought . . .

Bartleby!

He had to find Bartleby. He had to learn how to go back and change this now. Change what he had caused, through his own stupidity. Through his weakness. And make it all right.

He had to find Bartleby. But where to start? The college?

No, Nathan thought. Not yet. If he was going to look for him, then he should start where he had last seen him. *Where did I last see him? Where?*

Then he remembered.

The Underground!

CHAPTER TWENTY-FIVE

FOND MEETINGS

Bartleby wasn't in the Underground.

Nathan had ridden the trains for hours, to the Embankment and back, and around and around again, and back, and again. He had moved from car to car, changed seats, stared out of the windows at the stations passing by, waited. But nothing. Not even a glimpse of scarlet and black. Nor a flash of pike, or hat. Nothing.

He wandered the station, crossing from platform to platform, searching every corner, every elevator and escalator, every ticket kiosk and stall. There was no sign that a Beefeater had ever been there. Eventually he had to admit to himself that Bartleby was not in the Underground.

That left only one other place that he could think of.

He made his way to the college with a growing sense of despondency. He was beginning to think that things were irretrievable. What was done had become fixed, permanent. It could not be undone. The Moving Finger had finished its work.

He was not reassured one bit when he arrived and found the halls empty except for a few students wandering from class to the cafeteria. *Perhaps it's too early,* he thought. But in his heart he knew that it was not too early.

It was too late.

"How was your day, Nathan?" asked Godfrey as they walked together down the steps of the college. It was six o'clock. Bartleby had never shown.

Nathan could barely lift his spirits to answer, so he and Godfrey went to the car in silence. Godfrey opened the passenger door and, with a deep frown, watched Nathan get in.

"What is it, son?" he asked, climbing in behind the steering wheel. He started the engine. "You know, you've had a bit of a shock. You have to give it time."

Nathan turned. "Time?"

Godfrey nodded. "To get used to things again. Can't expect to get back into the swing of things all of a sudden. It's not only bones that need time to heal, is it?" He gave Nathan a friendly smile.

Nathan fastened his seat belt. "I guess so," he said politely. But he couldn't find it within him to smile back.

They were heading back toward Peckham High Street when Godfrey said, "Funny. You'll never guess what I saw at the college tonight."

Nathan said nothing. It wasn't that he was trying to be rude, he was just too upset to indulge in small talk. He watched the Christmas lights blink on and off outside instead.

"I said, you'll never guess what I saw at the college today, Nathan," Godfrey said. "Go on, guess!"

Nathan didn't rise to the bait.

"Go on, guess!"

"I don't know." Nathan sighed.

"No, go on. Take a guess!" urged Godfrey.

Nathan shrugged. "Santa Claus."

"No, come on."

Nathan wasn't in the mood for games. "I don't know," he said. "The Easter bunny? Mars and Jupiter? Two ten-foot chipmunks!"

Godfrey was a little put out by that. "All right, all right," he said, flustered. "I just thought you'd be interested . . . you know, because you mentioned it earlier."

"Mentioned it? Mentioned what?"

Godfrey nodded heavily. "The whatchamacallit," he said, struggling to recall the name. "The thingy. Big fella with the . . . er . . . you know. The doo-da!"

Nathan had almost given up listening.

"You know," Godfrey continued doggedly. "With the *pike*!"

Nathan's ears pricked up at that. He stared at the side of Godfrey's face. "A pike?"

"Yeah, that's right, isn't it?" Godfrey replied. "You know, that thingy that . . . er . . . wotsits carry. You know—"

Nathan was unable to restrain himself. "Beefeaters!" he yelled.

Godfrey broke into a wide, grateful smile. "Yeah, Beefeaters!"

Nathan grabbed Godfrey's shoulder. "Quick! Stop the car!" he called.

"What?"

"Stop the car, now!" repeated Nathan. "Stop, please!"

Godfrey braked quickly and swung the little Volkswagen to the curb. Before it came to a full stop, Nathan had opened the door.

"Nathan, wait!" Godfrey called as Nathan jumped out of the car. But Nathan was already across the road and running down the opposite sidewalk when he turned and shouted, "Tell Jan and Brian I'm sorry!"

He didn't stop until he'd reached the steps of New Cross Hill Community College.

"Bartleby!"

Inside the college, the halls were chillingly still and quiet. And dark. Nathan found the light switches and turned them on. "Bartleby!"

All at once the college filled with light. And there was a smell, clean and fresh.

"Bartleby!"

Nathan barreled on down the hallway, skidded around a corner, and barreled just as quickly down the next. And the one after that. He ran up the stairs, two at a time. Before too long he was outside the teachers' lounge door. He glanced in as he sprinted past. It was empty. But then, he knew it would be.

He knew now. He knew Bartleby was here, in the college. His grandfather. And he knew what he had to do.

He leaped down the stairwell. As his feet hit the ground with a *thud*, the lights blinked out suddenly. But Nathan ran on. His lungs were almost bursting when he saw the small circle of light in the shadows ahead. His feet clattered down the echoing halls, sounding out against the walls like gunshots. The circle of light bobbed.

And there was a voice in the darkness:

"You took your time!"

"Bartleby!" called Nathan, barely able to contain his joy. He laughed out loud as the circle of light picked out the Beefeater's extraordinary face. He was standing in the hallway, standing at attention as though he were at the Tower of London and the flashlight were nothing less than the crown jewels.

"Who did you expect?" answered Bartleby Cobb, grinning from ear to ear. "Santa Claus?"

The darkness reverberated with the sound of Nathan's footfalls and their laughter. Still, Nathan ran on. He was running so fast now that he could no longer feel the floor beneath his feet. He could no longer sense the walls around him, nor the ceiling. There was nothing but the darkness and Bartleby's smiling face. The same smile he'd seen in the photograph—his grandfather's smile.

Then there was a tremendous flash, as bright as a sun exploding. And a *bang*!

Then there was nothing.

CHAPTER TWENTY-SIX

NO PLACE LIKE HOME

" . . . for the longest time."

Nathan looked up from his bowl of cereal and blinked.

Henry was standing at the kitchen counter, eating a slice of burned toast and drinking from a cup of black coffee.

"What?" Nathan said.

"I said you've been staring at that bowl of cereal for the longest time," Henry repeated. "Are you all right?"

Nathan stared down at the cereal, at the notebook that was lying open on the table, at the spoon in his hand. He laughed to himself.

He was back. Back now. In the *real* now.

"Yes," he said. "I'm absolutely fine."

"Good," said Henry skeptically. He took a bite from the burned toast. "Anyway, like I say, he gets mixed up a lot with Chronos with an 'h.' *He's* the personification of time. But Cronos *without* an 'h' doesn't really have anything to do with time. He just ate his—"

"Dad?" said Nathan, interrupting.

"Yes, Nathan?"

Nathan smiled up at his father. *Henry*, he thought, *he's here! He's alive.*

Henry squirmed a little under Nathan's gaze.

"Nothing," Nathan said, shaking himself out of his torpor. He stood up from the table and grabbed his bag. "Well? Can we go?" he asked.

Henry was momentarily speechless. He had never known Nathan to be so eager to get to school. He held the toast and coffee absently. "Yeah," he said. "Okay."

"Oh, wait a minute," Nathan said. He ran to the kitchen drawer and pulled out a flashlight. Then, without pause, and holding it up like a lucky charm, he walked out of the apartment. "Come on," he said.

A bewildered Henry dropped his coffee and his toast on the counter and followed. He didn't know what to make of Nathan's unusual mood, but he wasn't going to risk anything that might puncture his enthusiasm. It had been a long time since he had seen him so excited and so motivated. He could only hope that it would last until the exams started.

Still, it was a little unnerving. And the way Nathan kept glancing at him made Henry imagine that he might disappear at any moment, or turn into a bat, or—

"It's not my hair, is it?" Henry asked later, when he was parking the Escort outside the school gates. He put his hand to his bald spot instinctively, and peered at his reflection in the rearview mirror.

"No, Dad," Nathan said, getting out of the car.

Henry waved heartily to Nathan as he walked through the school gates. Nathan waved back. Then Henry pulled away into the traffic, but not before one last glance at the mirror to check the size of his bald spot.

"What's that?" asked Moll.

They were in Mr. Scattergoods's class. Nathan was at his desk, the blue notebook open before him. He was staring intently at a blank page, smiling a long, sweet smile, as though he were staring at the most beautiful thing in the world.

Moll frowned at him. "You tied your tie too tight again, Nathan? Cut off the blood supply to your head?"

Nathan looked at her and began to laugh. He couldn't hide his joy at being back. He didn't want to. He was just happy to be here. To be here, with her, with Henry.

"Stop it," Moll hissed. "People are looking!"

There was a low rumble of chatter in the class, as the

other kids turned to stare at Nathan and Moll. Mr. Scattergoods glanced forgetfully at Nathan and tapped his ruler on the desk for quiet. But it was no good; Nathan couldn't help it. He had never been happier to be at school. He'd never been so happy to see Mr. Scattergoods, or to sit through double French. Or to see the blank page in his notebook. And he took out a pencil and began to draw a picture of a double-decker bus. It was a Routemaster. Number 230.

He was still smiling when Moll joined him in the cafeteria at lunchtime. He'd hardly touched his food. He was too excited. But the critical look in Moll's eye soon caused him to reign himself in a little.

"Did you ever know your mother, Moll?" he asked, when he had managed to stifle his smile enough to speak.

Moll paused briefly in picking with her fork at her food. "No," she said. "Dad said she just ran off one day. Went out for a loaf of bread and never came back."

"So it was just you and your dad?"

"Yeah," Moll said. "Until he disappeared."

Nathan glanced at the picture of the bus in his notebook. He thought of the Eckles and of Godfrey Pooter. He remembered the times on the common, with Fidget.

"Now it's just me," Moll said.

"*And* Jan. And Brian," Nathan corrected her.

Moll looked surprised. She hadn't realized she'd told Nathan so much about herself. Nice as it was, her foster family wasn't something she readily talked about. It was more than she wanted people to know.

"Anyway," Nathan added, thickening the outline of the bus with his pencil. "I've got a feeling it won't be long till you hear something about your dad."

"What do you mean?" asked Moll.

Nathan shut the notebook. Almost to himself, he said: "Oh, you know, a bump on the head. Shock can do funny things to the noggin, can't it?"

Moll looked at Nathan with the expression of someone who had looked up to see that the person sitting next to them was painted blue and singing, "I'm a little teapot, short and stout." She shook her head. "Yeah, Nathan," she said, "*whatever.*"

Nathan could only smile in reply.

"You going home?" Nathan asked, when they were standing together at the gates.

"Yeah," replied Moll. "What about you?"

"Oh, I've got a date with a Beefeater," said Nathan.

Most days an answer like that would have caused Moll to wonder whether she'd heard wrong, but not today. "You've been acting very weird," she said.

"I have?" Nathan grinned.

Moll considered the vague expression in his eyes for an instant. And Nathan considered the doubt in her face. A moment seemed to pass between them.

"Tomorrow's Saturday," said Nathan then, fighting the instinct to blush. "I thought maybe we could go see a movie or something? You know," he added, "*together*?"

Moll was silent. She flicked her hair out of her face and frowned, trying to figure out whether Nathan was joking or not. "All right," she said at last.

Nathan let out a relieved laugh. "Okay," he said. "I'll come by around lunchtime."

"You don't know where I live."

"I'll find you," Nathan said with unlikely confidence.

"Okay," Moll said, smiling. "See you, Nathan." She turned.

"Oh, and give my love to Jan and Brian," Nathan said.

He watched her as she walked down the street, joining the other kids. Everyone was headed home, back to civilization and TV. Everyone, that is, except Nathan. But he didn't care. Not now. He had something better than TV now.

And as the streetlights blinked on above Moll's head, burning like phosphorescent bars of pink soap, Nathan turned and headed to New Cross Hill, and to Mr. Hernandez's physics review class, for what he hoped would be the very last time.

CHAPTER TWENTY-SEVEN
THE MOVING FINGER WRITES

To Nathan's great surprise, he really enjoyed Mr. Hernandez's last class.

Finally, he thought, he had begun to understand the complicated ideas about relativity and time that Mr. Hernandez had been going on about all these weeks. And when the class ended and Mr. Hernandez's digital watch beeped to remind them that they were all free to go home, Nathan lingered. Before Mr. Hernandez had a chance to comment, Nathan told him: "I'll try to catch up in the future, sir."

"That's good, Nathan," Mr. Hernandez said, packing his briefcase.

"Oh, and you know what you said about time, sir?

Well, you were right, sir."

"I was?" Mr. Hernandez said, shuffling his papers absently.

"Yes," Nathan said, moving to the door. "The orange can be peeled, sir, but it can't be juiced. I know, I tried."

"Oranges?" repeated Mr. Hernandez, not quite taking it in.

"Oh, and don't worry," added Nathan, turning to go. "Nothing will be counter clockwise again, I promise. It's all hunky-dory—you'll see. But it's better not to brush your dogs' teeth tomorrow; another day won't do them any harm."

Mr. Hernandez blinked. "What?" he said, looking up from his briefcase.

But Nathan had already left.

He walked purposefully down the hallway, past the numerous classroom doors. The last time he had rushed, and outrun himself. *That was why I missed him,* he realized, because he had rushed and panicked. He wasn't going to make the same mistake again.

He reached the teachers' lounge just as the ceiling lights flickered.

"Right on the dot," he told himself, and quietly—as quietly as his hands could manage—he grasped the handle of the teachers' lounge door and turned it. It opened without a sound.

Nathan stepped inside, closing the door behind him. He got out the flashlight that he had taken from the kitchen drawer and switched it on. He aimed its light toward the floor.

In the armchair Godfrey Pooter was sleeping soundly. Quickly Nathan set to work untying the old gentleman's shoelaces. He hadn't a second to lose.

When it was done, he stood back and gave the scene one last satisfied look. Then he wiped his hands on his trousers and opened the door. Godfrey Pooter woke up at the sound of the handle.

"Hey, what's the joke?" said Godfrey.

Nathan threw him a wide-open smile. "You'll thank me for it later, Godfrey—honest!" he cried before closing the door behind him.

Godfrey's face crumpled in bewilderment. "I'll . . . I'll what?" he said, trying to pull himself up out of the chair. He reached for the door, but Nathan was halfway down the hallway by the time he had opened it. And Godfrey, stumbling over his shoelaces, fell through the doorway and straight into the arms of Enid Pidgin, who had only now managed to get her Nelson Turbo floor polisher to work and was at that very moment performing a figure eight by the teachers' lounge door.

Nathan turned in time to see dear old Enid carrying Godfrey off down the hallway astride her Nelson with all the grace of a ballerina on roller skates.

Next on the agenda was the school secretary's office.

Nathan got there just as the lights in the hallways flickered for a second time. He went inside and turned on the light. The office was empty: Bartleby wasn't there.

"Good," Nathan told himself. And he headed for the filing cabinet. Keeping an eye on the open door, he began to switch the files carefully, just as he had seen Bartleby do it—taking the contents of one file and placing them in a second file, and so on, until all the files were completely mixed up. When that was done, he turned to the photos pinned to the bulletin board. It was all fairly easy, and Nathan had to admit it was fun, too. And when it was over, he felt a burst of undisguised satisfaction at the work he had performed. He thought about all the lives he might have touched, and altered, by his deeds.

He checked to see that everything was as it *shouldn't* have been.

He was about to leave when he noticed something. He crossed to the desk, and with a cultured backhanded slice, he knocked the calendar into the wastepaper basket before turning off the lights and returning to the hall.

He waited. Quietly, to himself, he counted down the seconds.

Right on time the ceiling lights buzzed and crackled; then they blinked out altogether.

Nathan switched on the flashlight and walked across to the bottom of the stairs. Somewhere in the college he heard the sound of footsteps. They were coming closer. Soon something very large and very out of breath was coming down the steps toward him.

He aimed the flashlight up the stairs and watched it flare against the large blinking face of Bartleby Cobb. The Beefeater held up a thick, imposing hand to shield his eyes.

"Hey, that's not funny!" he called, but he was smiling nonetheless.

Nathan turned the beam to the ceiling. "What took you so long?" he asked, as Bartleby made his way carefully down the stairs. Nathan found the main switch and turned it on. Bartleby stood in full, glorious regalia under the fluorescent strip lights. He held out his arms and gave Nathan a big, bearlike hug. A long-lost hug. A grandfatherly hug. Then he held Nathan at arm's length in order to have a good look at him.

"How long do we have?" he asked.

"Plenty of time," Nathan said. "I've taken care of Godfrey."

"I noticed." Bartleby glanced at the bright red door of the secretary's office, and at the stairs. "And the office?"

"Done," said Nathan.

"Marvelous."

Then, with a leisurely wave of his ceremonial pike, he

and Nathan set off down the hallway, strolling like two old friends who had bumped into each other on the sidewalk. Just passing the time.

"Bartleby, there was something I wanted to ask you," Nathan said as they walked.

"Yes?"

"If it was you, Bartleby. If it was your wife who died, wouldn't you try to save her?"

Bartleby looked down ruefully. "It would do no good." He sighed.

Nathan nodded. Already he was feeling the tension of the moment and the gravity of what awaited him, only minutes from now. "Because of the Moving Finger?" he said.

Bartleby stopped. "Indeed, because of the Moving Finger. Some things are meant to happen, and there is nothing we can do to change them. Other things—things we have caused—may be set right *if* we have the courage to do so. There are so many separate times, Nathan, it is hard not to get lost in them." He glanced back at the stairs as though he had heard someone approaching. "Nathan," he said, "do you know how your parents met?"

Nathan thought about it. "No," he said, finally. "Dad's never mentioned it."

"By accident," Bartleby said. "That's how." He hesitated. "Or fate, or destiny," he added. "Or God's will—whatever you wish to call it. That is how we all meet and fall in love. And fall into hate. And it is how we die, when that time comes. It was Cornelle's time, Nathan, but it wasn't Henry's time."

Nathan understood that much now. "But why can't *you* stop him, Bartleby? Why come to me?"

"He wouldn't listen to me, Nathan. I let him down. I wasn't a good father, and he's never forgiven me. You see, he was always embarrassed by my job, my uniform. He wanted better for his mother and for himself. Besides—"

Nathan interrupted. "He doesn't know he's traveling through time, does he?"

Bartleby nodded, and Nathan recognized the admiration in his dark eyes. "You saw it?" asked Bartleby.

Nathan *had* seen it. At the Embankment. He'd seen the suspicion in Henry's face, the shock in his expression, and the guilt, pale and shining, like an illness. "He didn't even see me," Nathan said. "I was there, but he didn't see anything. Nothing but Mom—"

"That's what grief can do to a man. All he knows is he is lost, Nathan. At sea in a tragic memory. He doesn't know he's lost in time. He doesn't know and I don't want him to know. I want only for him to be happy again."

"But how? Mom, she's—"

"Time, Nathan," replied Bartleby. "Time heals all wounds. In time we all of us can overcome anything. Life or death. Believe me, I know." He smiled a ghostly sort of smile.

Nathan was about to say something more, but he was stopped by a noise from behind.

Bartleby pulled him into a narrow passageway. From there they watched as the figures of Godfrey Pooter and Enid Pidgin walked arm in arm down the stairwell, down the hall, and out to the exit. The pair had their heads bowed together, chatting—just as Bartleby had planned.

Nathan watched in awe. Once Enid and Godfrey had reached the exit and were standing there, talking and laughing, Nathan turned to Bartleby.

"But how do I stop him?" he whispered.

Bartleby's face was still, assured. "You'll find a way," was all he said.

There was the sound of a man's voice in the hall, and all at once Henry was at the doors to the college. Nathan saw him stop Godfrey, asking him if he'd seen his son.

"Nathan?" Henry called, turning from the old man, his voice echoing down the hall. "Nathan, you there?"

Nathan squeezed himself closer to Bartleby. "What I don't understand," he whispered, "is how Mr. Hernandez remembered me at the hospital. And Marbles. And how is it that I can remember both times?"

Bartleby smiled. "Have you heard of something called residual memory? It's like déjà vu, Nathan. Everyone feels it at times: that feeling that you have been here before. They say people who are vulnerable—say, if they've had a bump on the head—are more responsive to such things."

"*A shock can do funny things to the noggin,*" Nathan said.

"Indeed," Bartleby replied. "And animals, of course, are said to sense many things that humans cannot, like seeing ghosts, for example."

"That explains Marbles and Mr. Hernandez, but what about me?"

Bartleby put his hand on Nathan's shoulder and squeezed. "Perhaps you have a better reason to remember than most," he said. "Or perhaps it's in the blood," he added, glancing at Henry as he called out Nathan's name once more.

"Go on now," Bartleby said, "put him out of his misery."

"But will I see you again, Bartleby?"

"Perhaps. If you need me, you will."

Nathan could barely see the Beefeater's face now, for he had pressed himself harder against the wall, into the shadows, so that Henry would not notice him. He seemed suddenly smaller, almost mortal, standing there. *Faint,* Nathan thought. Like a memory that was fading with time. There was something terribly sad about seeing the great man hiding from his son.

"Good-bye, Nathan," Bartleby said.

"Good-bye, Grandpa."

Nathan embraced him one final time before walking out into the hall.

"There you are!" Henry called, seeing him, and he broke into a run. "I was worried I'd missed you," he said. "Sorry I'm late. There was gridlock. At the Embankment."

Nathan waited for Henry to approach. He wanted him to see Bartleby before they left for home—while he still had a chance—even if it was only for a moment. For Bartleby's sake.

But when Nathan looked back to the passageway, Bartleby had vanished.

CHAPTER TWENTY-EIGHT

THE WALL

"Death traps, those red Routemaster buses. . . . I don't care what you say, Nathan. The best thing they ever did was—" Henry stopped. He looked at Nathan, who sat silently staring at the side of his face.

"What is it?" Henry asked.

"Nothing," Nathan said. "You know, the Routemaster bus was particularly accident prone," he added. "In fact it averaged two fatalities a year. But it *was* nice and red, wasn't it?"

Henry tapped his ring finger in time to the song on the radio. "I suppose, if you like that sort of thing," he said. He glanced at the bus in his rearview mirror. A sense of vulnerability came over him then, and he concentrated very hard on the road and on the traffic, all the way to Tarside, and to the towers.

He parked the Escort in their spot by the garbage cans, and he and Nathan walked up to the steps of Tarside Heights, ignoring the burning Dumpster, which had been aflame now for twenty-six consecutive days. A record.

Nathan stared at the crane with its wrecking ball. It loomed against the sky like a monster, looking down upon Charlie and Turps, who were playing cards in a corner of the parking lot. Charlie was wearing a pirate's hat. He waved it as Nathan went by. Nathan waved back. Then he saw Marbles. He was shuffling out from under the tarpaulin. Nathan reached into his pocket, only to find that there was no chewing gum. There was only a rather chewed and worn tennis ball—one of Fidget's old ones—and he threw it to Marbles. The gray-faced pug sniffed at it disdainfully. He looked like he was about to rip it to shreds, but then something in his face softened. He gave it an exploratory chew, as though he recognized something in the smell, and he glanced up at Nathan, and Nathan could have sworn that he smiled. A lopsided, ugly sort of smile, but a smile nonetheless.

Nathan grinned. "Like the hat, Charlie!" he managed to say, before Henry ushered him inside the apartments.

"Dad, how did you and Mom meet?" Nathan asked as

the doors to the elevator opened. Henry looked steadily at Nathan. He was still staring when the elevator doors closed. They were almost up to the thirteenth floor before he answered.

"Why do you ask?" he said.

He unlocked the door of their apartment and walked straight down the hall and into the kitchen.

"I just wondered," said Nathan. He turned on the TV with the remote, but the whole time, he was looking at Henry from the corner of his eye. "You don't talk about her much."

"Well," Henry said, "it's difficult sometimes . . . thinking about your mother." Without another word he walked into the bathroom and started the shower.

Nathan waited. "I know," he said. He wouldn't have long to wait, he knew. And even as he spoke, Henry returned from the bathroom. "But how did you meet?" Nathan asked.

"It was an accident," started Henry, without looking up. "A long time ago," he added. "We were both heading down to the river. I'd already bought my ticket when she got on—"

"On?" echoed Nathan. "Were you on a train, Dad?"

Henry glanced up sharply, his eyes shining. He seemed startled. He'd never known Nathan to call him Dad before. "No," he said, a little unwillingly. "We were on the bus."

"A bus?" Nathan said, surprised. "A Routemaster?"

Henry nodded his head ruefully. "It was a long time ago, Nathan," he said. "There were only Routemasters back then. Me and your mom caught the same bus every morning. She got on at the stop after me. I'd noticed her before, but I'd never had the courage to talk to her."

Henry paused, remembering.

"Go on, Dad."

"Well," Henry said, "she bought her ticket from the conductor. The bus was packed and there was nowhere to sit. A car must have pulled out in front of us," he added, "because the bus braked suddenly and me and your mom fell forward. I caught her in my arms." Henry smiled to himself as the kettle boiled.

"Well, when the bus started again, we noticed that we'd dropped our tickets," Henry continued. "I saw them on the floor and picked them up, but they must have gotten mixed up."

"Mixed up?" asked Nathan.

Henry went to the bathroom to check on the shower. "I didn't notice until an inspector got on to inspect the tickets," he said, raising his voice so Nathan could hear. "Your mom had just gotten off the bus. Well, of course, I had the wrong ticket. I tried to explain, but the inspector wouldn't listen. He threw me off the bus!"

Nathan was listening in rapt silence. He'd never heard any of this before.

"Then I saw her," said Henry, appearing from the bathroom. "Your mom. She was running down the street from the previous stop. She'd noticed that she'd taken the wrong ticket and she was trying to catch up to the bus." He walked over to the kitchen counter and poured the water from the kettle into a cup.

"We just started talking, and that was that," he said, dipping his tea bag.

Nathan heard his father sigh. Heard the *plop* of the tea bag in the cup. He turned his head just enough to see—from the corner of his eye—Henry standing by the framed photo of Nathan's mom.

"So if it hadn't been for the mixup, or the bus braking," Nathan said, "then you'd never have met?"

There was a look of resignation on Henry's face. And Nathan began to worry. He was trying to act so normal—trying very hard to choose the right words.

"It was an accident, Dad," he said, getting up from the couch. "That's all."

Henry nodded gravely.

"Dad?" Nathan said, bracing himself. He took a step toward the bathroom door.

On the TV the man on the news was saying that a new species of mule had been found in Borneo that could speak Esperanto. . . .

"It wasn't your fault, Dad," Nathan cried, but already

Henry was heading for the bathroom. Before Nathan could stop him, he'd run inside and banged the door shut, and a bright white light flashed beneath the bottom of the door.

"Dad!"

Nathan was in the bathroom before the flash had died away. He could see the figure of his father outlined against the white light. He was hanging like a puppet, in time.

In the split second before Henry was torn from the bathroom, Nathan grabbed his hand and held on. There was a great *bang* as the rear wall smashed apart.

And they were gone. Nathan and Henry together.

Gone. Through the wall.

CHAPTER TWENTY-NINE
ONLY A SMALL INCIDENT

The Christmas lights were shining brightly on the Embankment.

They sparked and fizzed like glass fireworks while below them the cars pulled to a halt. There was a traffic jam ahead.

Nathan opened his eyes. He was cold and wet, and his fingers hurt from clinging so tightly to his father's sleeve. Henry was there too, crouching on the sidewalk some yards away, trying hard not to be crushed in the charge of the afternoon crowds.

The car headlights shone fiercely against the falling snow, like fire. But the snow would pass, Nathan told himself, standing up. It always did.

The sidewalks were bustling with people running blind, trying to escape the snowfall, and by the time Nathan had struggled upright and looked to see where Henry was, he was already staggering down the sidewalk, his suit torn at the elbow, his trousers wet from the rain.

"Dad!" Nathan shouted, starting after him. But he had barely set off when he lost his footing on the wet sidewalk. He fell. For a moment the glare of the headlights from the traffic blinded him. He imagined he saw, far down the road, a green coat like the one his mother wore.

Then he saw the bus drive by.

"Dad!" Nathan yelled, struggling to his feet. He pushed past the crowd.

"Watch it," said one of the passersby.

"Careful," warned another.

"Mind yourself, kid!"

Nathan was deaf to them all. In the distance he glimpsed Henry's balding head bobbing in the crowd.

How did he get so far away so quickly? How had Nathan let him escape?

The bus rumbled on down the road. The rain began to lash down. The headlights flashed. And Henry. Henry ran blind, down from the sidewalk and across the road, into the oncoming traffic. Seeing him, the drivers of the cars screeched to a halt or swerved to miss him. They skidded and fishtailed, but miraculously, there was no collision. Henry stumbled on, reaching the safety of the opposite sidewalk just as the bus drove past.

Nathan had no choice but to follow. As the cars maneuvered back into their lanes, he dashed between them and raced after Henry and the bus. Henry was slowing and so was the bus. The traffic was getting heavier the farther down the road they went. Before too long Nathan was no more than ten yards away from Henry. He was close enough now to see his face as he peered up to scrutinize the bus beside him. *He looks awful,* thought Nathan, hollowed out, as though he hadn't slept for weeks. His eyes were wild and his mouth gaped open. Set against the red of the bus Henry appeared pale, ghostly.

Nathan was almost within reach of him when Henry set off again, spurred on by the sight of something in the distance.

It was Cornelle. She was standing at a mailbox. Briefly, Nathan saw a blue envelope in her hand before she slipped it into the mouth of the box.

Her hair was wet with the rain, and she was wearing the green coat with the fake fur collar that Henry had bought her for her birthday.

As he watched, she turned and reached in her bag for her umbrella as the rain began to come down harder. Henry ran for her, Nathan ran toward Henry. The bus only accelerated harder.

Henry was fast, but Nathan was faster. He was catching up now as Henry began to lose his balance. When he tumbled to the ground, Nathan was there, catching his arm.

"Dad!" he said, holding him.

Henry's wild eyes flashed on Nathan. For a moment he didn't recognize him; then the awful truth of the moment seemed to dawn. He looked from Nathan to Cornelle. If only Cornelle had looked up, she would have seen them standing there together, holding each other. But she was too busy trying to get her umbrella to open.

The bus approached. The sunlight bounced up from the puddles in the road and what was left of the snow.

A low sob came out of Henry's chest as Nathan clung to him. He tried to pull away, but Nathan was just as determined and just as strong.

"Dad. Dad, stop!" gasped Nathan, holding on.

Henry dropped to the ground.

Cornelle had the umbrella open now. She'd stepped into the road without having looked up. Without having noticed the bus for the rain.

Henry and Nathan watched it all. Time seemed to slow. They saw the bus, and they saw the umbrella. . . . *The Moving Finger writes; and, having writ, Moves on . . .*

They saw the bus begin to brake, saw Cornelle look up, too late . . . *nor all your Piety nor Wit Shall lure it back to cancel half a Line* . . . And in the distance, in the rain, they saw Cornelle half turn, as if she had heard her name called. She looked around, not knowing who might have called out, and then . . . time . . .

. . . stopped.

Her eyes met theirs.

She saw Henry and Nathan standing together. It was the last thing she would ever see, her son and his father together, as they should be, for eternity.

And she *smiled*, because it was all she had wished for, and all she could want, now: Henry and Nathan together.

They never heard the *bang*. They didn't see the ambulance arriving or the crowd gathering in the street. They never heard the sound of the sirens or the gasp of the onlookers. They saw only her eyes on theirs. They saw her face and knew they would never, ever forget it. They saw only the sunlight against her skin, and the kindness there, like a new light all of its own. They saw only her smile.

Then nothing for the longest time.

. . . *Nor all your Tears wash out a Word of it*. . . .

CHAPTER THIRTY

THE RAVENS RETURN

The page was blank.

No matter how long he stared at it, nothing appeared. Nathan had never dreamed of a blank page before. It had always been dinosaurs or armies at war or volcanoes spewing lava. But never a blank page. He wondered what it could mean. He knew blood was a sign of an agitated mind. He knew water meant strong emotions. But a blank page? Did it mean anything at all? Or was it just blank?

When he woke, for a few fleeting moments he remembered what he had dreamed, and then it was gone from his mind, the way dreams do sometimes, never to be recaptured. He woke with a bright light on his face, and he imagined he was in the hospital again. He felt for his arm, but there was no cast, and no bones were broken; and the light on his face was only the sun streaming in through the window of his bedroom. *His* bedroom in Tarside Heights, the same as always. There were some old comics scattered around on the floor. A pile of dirty clothes sat in one corner of the room, and in another was a broken bike that Nathan had found but had never gotten around to fixing. The same.

He climbed out of bed and found he was already dressed in his school uniform. Or rather, that he hadn't undressed the night before. The uniform was crumpled and creased, and it didn't smell too good either. He went to the chest of drawers, pulled out his spare school shirt, and changed into it. Almost at once he felt better, more awake.

He opened the bedroom door and stepped out. It was quiet. He wondered what time it was, but thought better of looking at his watch. He had had enough of watches to last him two lifetimes.

"Dad?" he called. "Henry?"

No answer.

He looked in the kitchen. Then he looked in the bathroom. The rear wall of the bathroom was good and solid—there was no hole. But there was no Henry, either.

"Dad?" he said, opening the door to his father's bedroom and going inside. The curtains were open and the bed was made. No Henry.

Nathan was beginning to worry when he heard the door of the flat open.

"Dad?" he asked timidly.

"Who did you expect," answered Henry, walking through the door, "Santa Claus?" He was carrying a loaf of bread in one hand and a bunch of letters in the other, and there was a newspaper tucked under his arm. "Breakfast, Nathan?" he asked.

"Yes, thanks," Nathan said.

Henry went to the kitchen and switched on the kettle. "You ready for school already?" he asked.

"Um, yes," replied Nathan. "Thought I'd get dressed early."

"I'll say," said Henry. "It's Saturday today. You're two days early."

Nathan frowned. "Oh."

He hadn't realized. It seemed to him that it had been the same day all week long, over and over again. He had totally forgotten that it would end.

"What's that?" Nathan asked, nodding at Henry's hand.

"This?" asked Henry, lifting the loaf of bread. "This is a loaf of bread, Nathan, son. Very handy for making toast. Essential, you might say."

Nathan shrugged. "No," he said, "I mean that!" He pointed at Henry's other hand, at the bunch of envelopes.

"Oh, these? Load of mail that got lost in transit. Mailman just delivered it now. Funny guy, very nervous. Says he's been trying to deliver them for days. Some of these go back years, though," he said, sifting through them on the counter. Then he stopped. He went a little pale. He picked out a particular envelope, a small, neat blue one with a handwritten address on it.

Nathan recognized it immediately. It was Cornelle's letter. It had finally arrived.

Holding it in his hand, Henry moved to the table. He slumped down on the chair as though his legs had given in.

"You okay, Dad?" Nathan asked.

Henry looked up at him, glassy eyed. "Yeah, fine, Nathan," he said. There was something new in his eyes. They were no longer hollow or empty. *They seem alive again,* thought Nathan. "Why don't you go and change, Nathan?" Henry said. He waited with the envelope in his hands until Nathan had walked back to his room.

Through the crack between the door and the frame, Nathan saw him begin to open the envelope, so carefully. His fingers slid in and took out the letter. He unfolded it. When he had finished reading it, his head dropped and he began to cry. Nathan closed the door, leaving Henry to his own memories. Then he went to change his clothes.

"Anything interesting, Dad?" Nathan asked, once he was dressed in a fresh shirt and pants. He had waited ten minutes or more, wanting to make sure that Henry had had time to gather his thoughts, and then he had opened his door.

"What?"

Henry was standing in the kitchen. There were five or six torn brown envelopes and their corresponding letters laid out on the counter, and Nathan could see Cornelle's blue envelope tucked in the back pocket of Henry's trousers. Henry had made himself a cup of bitter black coffee, and he took a sip of it as Nathan joined him.

"Ooh," he groaned, his ulcers grumbling. "Might have a cup of tea instead." And he poured the coffee down the sink.

"Why not have some orange juice?" Nathan said, opening the fridge and removing a carton of juice. "And some cereal?"

"Okay," Henry said. "Yes, why not?" He paused. "I was just thinking that I'd better start taking care of myself," he said. "I'm not getting any younger, am I? After all, my first duty is to stay safe and healthy, isn't it?" he said, somewhat stiffly. "I mean, so I can be a good father."

There was an awkward silence as Henry took a sip of the freshly poured orange juice. "Mmm," he said, finally—and rather unconvincingly. "Sorry, what did you say, Nathan?"

"Was there anything interesting in the mail?"

"Oh, yes. There was. Seems like we've got somewhere to live after all," Henry said cheerfully.

Henry picked up one of the official-looking letters from the counter and handed it to Nathan. "They've found us a place over in Friar's Court. Nice place. Letter must have got lost in the mail, with the rest of it. Maybe things are looking up," he said. There was an expression of profound relief on Henry's face that was not due solely to the news about their new home.

He really does look like a transformed man, Nathan thought. Like a great weight had been lifted from his shoulders. He even looked a little younger.

"We'd just had lunch together, you know," Henry said all of a sudden. Henry had walked across to the window. The curtains were open and he was staring out into the distance, to the blurred horizon of the city. "Your mom and me. That day at the Embankment. You know, we were thinking of getting back together," he said, and he removed the blue envelope from his back pocket and glanced at it. His eyes looked wet.

"Oh, that reminds me!" he said. And he dashed at once into his bedroom. When he returned, he was holding a photograph in his hand. He offered it to Nathan. "Here," he said.

It was an old, creased black-and-white photograph of a

very large, very heavy-looking Beefeater. He was holding his ceremonial pike in one hand, and in his free arm he was cradling a small baby.

"It's Bartleby," gasped Nathan, before he could stop himself.

"Yes," said Henry. If he was surprised that Nathan knew the name, he didn't show it. "You were asking about Grandpa Cobb. It's the only photo I have. It was taken not long before he died. I thought you might like to have it. Here," he said, pointing to the little baby in Bartleby's arm. "That's you!"

"Me?"

"Of course. He liked *you,* Nathan," Henry said. "In fact, I think you are probably the only thing I've ever done in my life that he approved of."

Nathan stared at the photograph, considered the happiness and the mystery in the old Beefeater's face, his grandfather. "Thanks," he said.

"That's all right, Nathan," Henry said. He sipped his orange juice. "I was thinking this afternoon we could go and do something together, son," he added. "The movies maybe, or bowling. What do you say?"

Nathan looked up from the photo. "Can't today, Dad," he said. "I've kind of . . . got a date."

"Oh."

"In fact I'd better get going," he said. "I've got to get over to Moll's place, on Acacia Avenue. Can I take this with me?" he said, holding up the photo.

"Course you can. Just take care of it, okay?" Henry said. "Acacia Avenue?" he asked. "I'll drive you there. Is it far?"

"Not far," Nathan said.

Henry nodded. "Okay, let's go," he said, putting down his empty glass and picking up his car keys. "Pity about the movies, though."

"But we could do something tomorrow," Nathan added hastily. "Unless you think I should be studying?"

Henry laughed. "There'll be time later for studying, Nathan. Anyway, I never got any qualifications, and look at me! Best soap seller in the metropolitan area!"

Nathan laughed too. Then Henry went to the door and opened it.

"Aren't they turning on the Christmas lights tonight?" he asked. "We could stay up and watch them."

"Great," Nathan said. "But maybe we should get some candles," he added. "I heard there might be a power outage." He walked out of the door and toward the elevator. "And maybe tomorrow we could go down to the river, Dad. Go on a boat? And then we could go to the Tower of London and take a look at the ravens? If we've got time?"

Henry glanced once around the apartment, to check that everything was turned off and everything was safe.

He felt for the blue envelope in his pocket. Then he went out. "Oh, I'm sure we've got time, Nathan," he said, shutting the door behind him. "We've got all the time in the world."